"Are you hiding? Or are you the plant inspector?"

Molly froze. With as much dignity as she could muster, she pulled her head from between the plastic branches and turned to face the man.

"Of course I'm hiding," she whispered.

"Who are you hiding from?" His easy tone was laced with humor.

"See that man over there?" she said in a low voice as he bent to peer through the plant.

He followed her gaze. The man was leaning against a far wall, twitching nervously. He was short and bald, and apparently he had misplaced his chin, causing the fuzzy growth of his beard to sprout from somewhere in his neck. What little hair he did have was gray and worn long, grazing the collar of his plaid polyester sports coat.

"That one?" He turned to her, his deep voice filled with disbelief. "Who is he?"

"That man is . . . Jonathan Kent, my blind date."

Dear Reader,

Welcome to Silhouette. Experience the magic of the wonderful world where two people fall in love. Meet heroines who will make you cheer for their happiness, and heroes (be they the boy next door or a handsome, mysterious stranger) who will win your heart. Silhouette Romances reflect the magic of love—sweeping you away with books that will make you laugh and cry, heartwarming, poignant stories that will move you time and time again.

In the next few months, we're publishing romances by many of your all-time favorites, such as Diana Palmer, Brittany Young, Emilie Richards and Arlene James. Your response to these authors and other authors of Silhouette Romances has served as a touchstone for us, and we're pleased to bring you more books with Silhouette's distinctive medley of charm, wit and—above all—*romance*.

I hope you enjoy this book and the many stories to come. Experience the magic!

Sincerely,

Tara Hughes
Senior Editor
Silhouette Books

SHARON DE VITA
Heavenly Match

Published by Silhouette Books New York

America's Publisher of Contemporary Romance

To my husband Tony:
After seventeen years, my only regret
is that we have but a lifetime together.

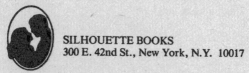

SILHOUETTE BOOKS
300 E. 42nd St., New York, N.Y. 10017

Copyright © 1986 by Sharon De Vita

ISBN: 0-373-08475-7

First Silhouette Books printing December 1986

America's Publisher of Contemporary Romance

Printed in the U.S.A.

SHARON DE VITA

has been happily married to her high school sweetheart for seventeen years. To be published was a lifelong dream of hers. Sharon lives in Downers Grove, Illinois, with her husband and three children. She firmly believes in happy endings.

Chicago •
Hillchester •

ILLINOIS

ILLINOIS
Underlined places are fictitious.

Chapter One

Why, oh why, had she ever let her aunt talk her into this blind date? Molly wondered wildly. Carefully hidden behind a towering plastic fern, she had a clear view of the man. Even though he was halfway across the crowded restaurant, Molly was certain it was *him*!

Groaning softly, she gratefully accepted a complimentary glass of champagne from a passing waiter before parting the plastic branches for another peek at her date.

Lord, on second glance, it was even worse than she had first thought! Molly desperately downed her champagne. The man was leaning against a far wall, twitching nervously. He was short and bald, with the droopiest eyes this side of a basset hound. His skin was milky white, and apparently he had misplaced his chin, since his fuzzy growth of beard appeared to sprout from somewhere in his neck. What little hair he did have was gray and worn long; it hung limply down the back of his egg-shaped head, grazing the collar of his plaid polyester sports coat.

Molly frowned. What the devil was the matter with his pants? She craned her neck for a better look, and her sapphire eyes widened in horror. Lord, the man had shrunk his pants! The trousers, which were a riotous shade of lime green, stopped just above his ankles to reveal a pair of faded yellow sports socks. At least both his shoes appeared to match, Molly thought, as she grabbed another glass of champagne.

She sighed deeply as her eyes took him in. At least her aunt had been right about one thing: Jonathan Kent, Molly's blind date, did look exactly like his eighty-five-year-old grandmother!

"Are you hiding, or are you the plant inspector?"

Molly froze. The rich masculine voice was just close enough and soft enough to skate along her nerve endings, jerking her to attention. With as much dignity as she could muster, she pulled her head from between the plastic branches and turned to face the man. Her eyes went directly to the shock of copper hair atop his head. He looks like a fire hydrant, she thought giddily. The fiery curls were combed neatly, but several strands fell across his forehead, giving him a somewhat boyish look.

But this was no boy, Molly realized with a jolt as her eyes traveled to his face. And what a face, she thought dizzily: deep aquamarine eyes, a straight proud nose and a full mouth that was just made for kissing. As her gaze toured the length of him, she became aware of the width of his shoulders and his long lean frame. He towered over her five-foot-three frame, and she wasn't at all certain the immaculate gray, pin-striped suit he wore wasn't painted on; it molded his sculptured body perfectly, outlining every muscle, every bulge.

Blushing, Molly pulled her eyes up to a more respectable level. She stiffened. *His* eyes were doing a little touring of their own. She suddenly wished she had taken her aunt's advice and left a few buttons open at the neck of her dress. And it certainly wouldn't have hurt to have let her dark brown hair fall loose to her shoulders. The crisp French braid was fine for work, but somehow, with this man's eyes on her, the last thing she wanted to look like was a prim and proper kindergarten teacher. Why, oh why, hadn't she listened to her aunt and advertised her "wares" a little more?

"Are you hiding?" he repeated with a lopsided grin.

"Of course, I'm hiding," she whispered, lost in his eyes. They were fabulous—tiny flecks of green amid a sea of rich, deep blue.

"Who are you hiding from?" His easy tone was laced with humor.

"Not who," she corrected. "Whom."

"Whom?"

"*Whom* are you hiding from?"

He chuckled softly, then threw up his hands. "I give up. Whom are you hiding from?"

Molly smiled weakly. "I don't know."

His amber brows rose, and a smile twitched at the corners of his mouth. "You don't know?"

"That's right." Molly frowned. Was he dense? She'd just explained that to him, hadn't she? She reached out to grab another glass of champagne from a passing waiter, but a large, warm hand reached out and stopped her.

"Oh, no you don't. I think you've had quite enough to drink. I'm not even sure you're old enough to drink."

His eyes slid over her again, and Molly shivered. His look made her feel more lightheaded than the champagne.

Noting the sudden mischief dancing in his eyes, Molly yanked her hand free and tried to garner some feminine dignity. "For your information, sir, I am quite old enough to drink. And," she added boldly, lifting her empty glass in the air, "old enough to do a great many other things."

"I see," he murmured, struggling to look somber. "You're old enough to drink and do a great many other things. You're hiding, but you don't know from whom." He scratched his head in obvious confusion. "Have I got all of this so far?"

Molly smiled. "Got it."

A fresh grin trembled across his lips. "Good. At least we're making progress, I think. Now, where do we go from here?" His brows rose expectantly as Molly parted the plastic branches for him.

"See that man over there?" she whispered, as he bent his long frame to peer through the plant. His face was so close that she could feel the warmth of his breath on her neck, and a heated shiver ran down her spine.

"That one?" He turned to her, his masculine voice filled with disbelief.

"That's the one." Molly nodded dismally, then took a deep breath. The scent of his after-shave was positively heavenly. Woodsy with a hint of pine, it caressed her dazed senses like a warm breeze. "What are you wearing?" she asked absently. "It smells wonderful." Her lids fluttered closed for a moment, and she swayed, not certain if it was from the champagne or from the man standing next to her.

"Whoa, easy." He dropped his hands to her shoulders to steady her, but his touch had just the opposite effect, and Molly swayed again. Swallowing hard, she took another deep breath, savoring the scent of him.

"Easy, girl." His grin widened and his eyes twinkled. "Now, what about that man? Why are we hiding from him? And why on earth are we whispering?" He straightened his long frame, and Molly had to tilt her head back to look at him. A pleasurable experience, she decided as a jolt skidded along her spine.

"I'm not hiding, not really. I don't even know that man. Not yet, anyway." Molly frowned. He was grinning down at her again.

"Come on, pretty lady. What you need is some fresh air. It will help clear your head." He grabbed her hand and started pulling her through the restaurant.

"No, wait!" she yelped. "He'll see me."

He stopped abruptly and stared at her, his face a study in confusion. "Who'll see you?"

This one was handsome, but dense. "That man," she repeated with forced patience. "He'll see me."

"But I thought you just said you didn't know—that you weren't hiding— Never mind." Laughing, he shook his head. "Come on, you need that fresh air a lot more than I thought. Let's go stand by the back door. I think it's open. That way no one will see us." Before she could protest, he spun on his heel, tugging her along behind him.

The cool, fresh air hit Molly square in the face, and she took a deep, shaky breath, vividly aware that he was still holding her hand. His fingers, wrapped gently around hers, were having a strange effect on her inner system.

"Feeling better?" he queried, watching as she took large gulps of fresh air.

"Much," she lied, feeling anything but better. The sudden rush of air to her lungs did little to soften the impact this man was having on her.

"Now how about an explanation? One piece at a time, please." His brows rose hopefully and Molly's heart sank. What could she tell him? That her dear, sweet, well-intentioned aunt had a nasty habit of corralling any moving thing in pants in an effort to find a man for her? No, she certainly couldn't tell him that.

"The man inside? You do remember who he is, don't you?" His brows drew together, and Molly shifted uncomfortably, a weak smile on her face.

"Oh yes," she murmured, "the man inside." How could she forget? At the moment she gladly would have strangled Aunt Emily. How could she tell this man that her aunt arranged her dates? Getting a man wasn't a problem; keeping Aunt Emily from getting her one was!

Gathering her dwindling courage, Molly took a deep breath and lifted her chin. "That man inside is... Jonathan Kent. My blind date." A sigh of relief escaped her. There! The words were out, but she hardly recognized the hoarse whisper as her own.

"Your what?" His mouth was twitching, and Molly heaved an exasperated sigh.

"Blind date," she repeated. Shaking her head numbly, Molly sought to put some words together. "My aunt arranged a blind date for me with the grandson of her best friend. I wasn't hiding from— I wanted a chance to— I just—" Molly stopped as a deep chuckle broke loose from his broad chest.

Glaring at him, Molly resisted the urge to give him a good whack. It certainly wasn't all that funny!

"Tell me," he managed to get out, "how did you pick out this . . ."

"Kent," she supplied stiffly. "Jonathan Kent."

"This Kent fellow from the crowd?"

Molly scowled. "That was easy. My aunt said he looked just like his grandmother." A small whimper escaped her lips. "She was right."

"I see." He looked into her eyes, and Molly could tell he didn't see, not at all.

"Look, I really have to be going now. I certainly don't want to keep my date waiting." That was certainly a lie, she thought grimly. She didn't care if Johnathan Kent waited until the rest of his hair fell out. Judging from the looks of the man, that just might be momentarily.

Molly turned, fully intending to leave the grinning redheaded giant standing there, but he reached out and stopped her.

"Hey, wait a minute. I have a wonderful idea." He rocked back on his heels and smiled down at her, causing Molly to take a step back. From the look on his face, she had a feeling his idea was not going to be all that wonderful.

"No, really, it's a wonderful idea," he assured her as he bent his head to whisper in her ear. "Why don't we just leave? No one will have to know. *I* can be your blind date for tonight." His sweet breath caressed her ear, sending a pulsing shaft of pleasure through her limbs. The idea was just deliciously reckless enough to warrant momentary consideration. But then her senses righted. What would she tell her aunt? That she just happened to pick up a strange man in the bar? No, that would never do.

Hesitantly she lifted her eyes to his. He was so close that she could see the tiny laugh lines around his eyes, see the light dusting of fawn-colored freckles across his nose, see the way his soft mouth gently sloped upward. Molly blinked. His nearness was doing strange things to her.

"That's—that's just not possible," she stammered, unable to drag her eyes from his. "In the first place it would be..." Molly closed her eyes. Wonderful, she thought silently. "Rude," she gasped aloud, startled by the train of her traitorous thoughts. "Yes, it would be incredibly rude. And in the second place..." Molly looked up at him and her thoughts scattered like leaves in a brisk fall wind. She'd think of another good reason in a moment, she was almost sure of it.

"And in the second place?" he queried gently.

"Um... I already have a date." Lord, her date! She was out here fantasizing about running off into the night with a perfect stranger, and Jonathan Kent was probably twitching around the four corners of the restaurant looking for her. "Look, I really have to go now," she muttered, backing up a bit. Turning, she fled back into the restaurant, pausing for a moment in the washroom to compose herself.

Were there no gentlemen left in the world? she wondered miserably. First, she'd gotten matched with a man better suited to a bulldog. Then she'd had the dismal misfortune of meeting a man who'd assumed she was the type of woman to slip off ito the night with a perfect stranger. A wistful smile curved her lips. She had to admit, the redheaded stranger *was* perfect in every detail. That smile was the most glorious, nerve-splitting smile she had ever seen. And those eyes. Molly sighed dreamily. He had a way of looking at her that made her feel as if she were the only person in the world. His world, at least.

Her spirits dropped and an unwelcome tension tightened her shoulders. No use daydreaming about a man she would probably never see again. Right now she had more pressing problems, like how she was going to get through the evening with Jonathan Kent.

Molly shook her head. Ever since Molly had broken her engagement the year before, her aunt had been hauling men home like wayward strays, hoping to find a good one for her. She was perfectly happy with her job as a kindergarten teacher and with her pet cat, Nickodemus, and, of course, with Aunt Emily. A man would only complicate things. Besides, she had learned her lesson. Long ago she'd realized that men were nice as long as they didn't get close enough to hurt her. Molly took pains to make sure that none ever did.

Her expression darkened and she scowled at her reflection. One thing was certain: this was going to be a very early evening. The sooner it was over the better. At least she wouldn't have to worry about faking a headache tonight, because she suddenly had a ferocious one.

Winding her way through the crowded restaurant again, Molly was relieved to find that her blind date was nowhere to be found. Maybe he's left, she thought hopefully as she approached the maître d'.

"Hello, I'm Molly Maguire. I'm here to meet—"

"Yes, of course, right this way." He dutifully cupped her elbow as he led her through the crowded dining room. "Here we are, Miss Maguire." He motioned her to a booth.

Might as well get this over with, Molly thought, plastering a tight smile on her face. She deliberately kept her eyes down as she slid into the booth. "I'm Molly

Maguire," she said with exaggerated brightness. When she forced herself to look at the man opposite her, the breath rushed from her lungs. "You!" It was him! The redheaded giant that had tried to get her to slip off with him.

"Hello, again." He gave her a mock salute that ignited her temper. Molly's jaw clamped stubbornly, and she glared at him across the table.

"If this is your idea of a joke, I don't think it's very funny. I already told you, I have a date!" Lord, why her? Groaning softly, Molly started to slide out of the booth, but she froze as her eyes settled on Jonathan Kent. He was tottering toward them, swiveling his egg-shaped head in every direction. He's looking for me, Molly thought in a panic. Her heart gave a lurch, and her pulse danced into double time.

"You!" she whispered to the redheaded giant. "I have to get rid of you. You have to hide."

"Hide?" he repeated innocently.

"Don't tell me you're hard of hearing on top of everything else." When he made no attempt to move, Molly lifted the delicate lace tablecloth and peered underneath. No, he'd never fit under the table, at least not without being noticed. If it wasn't for those darn long legs she might have been able to squeeze him in.

"May I ask what you're doing?" he asked with maddening calm.

"Trying to find someplace to hide you," she snapped.

"How about in here?" He picked up her small clutch purse and waved it under her nose. She snatched it from his hand, sorely tempted to try and stuff him into it.

"This is all your fault," she whispered fiercely as her blind date approached. What on earth was she going to tell Jonathan Kent? That she brought along a spare man just in case he didn't work out? What a mess!

Never, ever again, would she go out on another date, blind or otherwise! She darted a glance at the man sitting across from her. He was totally calm and seemingly oblivious to her panic. Why didn't he just go away and leave her alone in her misery? She couldn't handle one man, let alone two!

Nervously biting her lip, Molly made a conscious effort to calm down. She'd just have to tell the truth. She'd simply have to explain to Jonathan Kent that the man wouldn't leave her alone.

The bald-headed man tottered past her without even glancing in her direction. Startled, Molly gaped after him.

"Excuse me, but if you're through playing hide-and-seek, I'd like to introduce myself."

Molly's head snapped around at the rich laughter in his voice. Her eyes met his, and for an instant she thought she might faint. "You?" she asked weakly. "Don't tell me *you're* Jonathan Kent!"

Chapter Two

"Molly? It is Molly, isn't it?"

His teasing tone only added to her embarrassment, and Molly's cheeks burned. The first time her aunt had fixed her up with a handsome, normal man, she'd behaved like a mindless twit! What on earth must the man think of her? There were several possibilities, she realized. He probably thought she was drunk or demented. Possibly both!

A spark of anger penetrated her embarrassment. It was just as much his fault as hers. Molly lifted her head, sapphire eyes blazing. "Why the devil didn't you just tell me who you were?"

With his eyes intent on her, Jonathan stretched his long frame, then settled back comfortably against the booth. "You really didn't give me much chance. You were too busy trying to dodge Mr. Egghead."

Did he have to remind her? she wondered miserably. Reluctantly, she had to admit what he said was true. She really hadn't given him much chance to explain. She'd never suspected that Jonathan was— How on earth could she have known? Jonathan Kent was not like any blind date she'd ever encountered.

Molly gave him a weak smile, hoping to make amends. "Look, Jonathan, I'm sorry. I had no idea— It never occurred to me that you—" Her voice broke as her thoughts scattered. Did he have to stare at her so intently? It made it nearly impossible to think, let alone speak.

"You were saying, Molly?" The edges of his mouth curled and she found herself flushing hotly again.

"Well, how the devil was I supposed to know that you were you? You don't even resemble your grandmother!"

"But that other man did?" Jonathan's brows rose, and he chuckled softly. "Wait until I tell my grandmother," he threatened gleefully, wagging a finger at her.

"You wouldn't dare!" Molly gasped, horrified. Even in her distress she found the man's impact stirring. When he looked at her with those laughing eyes, she felt like ice cream on a hot August day: warm and melting.

"What else do you know about me besides the fact that I don't look like my grandmother?"

Molly stared at him, desperately trying to recall just exactly what Aunt Emily had told her about him. The only thing she could remember was that Jonathan Kent was supposed to be a very nice boy. Boy, indeed!

"Not much, really," she murmured, nervously taking a sip of her water. It was much easier to think if she didn't have to look directly into his eyes.

"Molly?" Something in his voice caused her to lift her eyes to his, and she instantly regretted it as her heart flipped.

"That's better. I like to see your eyes when I talk to you. Did you know your eyes are very expressive?" His voice dropped to a husky whisper, and her pulse hammered. "I can tell a lot about a person by their eyes."

Her breath caught in her lungs, and her confidence dropped another notch. Lord, she hoped the man couldn't read minds, too. Refusing to give in to the discomfort that was tracking her, Molly forced herself to keep her eyes on his, even if it did make her breathing come faster.

"Shall I fill in the blanks?"

"Blanks?" she echoed dully. Somehow she had lost the thread of the conversation.

"Yes. You know, vital statistics and things?"

Molly nodded and forced herself to pay attention to Jonathan's words and not to the quickening of her heart.

"I'm an attorney for a large real estate conglomerate in Portland, Oregon. The firm I work for specializes in commercial and industrial properties. I've lived in Portland for about twelve years and try to get home at least twice a year to see my grandmother. I'm thirty-five, single, wear a size thirty-eight long suit and size eleven shoe. I prefer striped ties to prints. I'm left-handed and extremely allergic to fur. I wear glasses only for reading and have been inoculated against all major diseases." Jonathan smiled at her. "Have I left anything out?"

Molly shook her head in amazement, trying to digest the catalog of information. "Just what color pajamas you wear?" she muttered.

"I don't wear pajamas," he said softly. "How about you?" He grinned mischievously, and Molly's cheeks burned. Why on earth hadn't she asked what color socks he wore!

A waiter approached, and she sighed gratefully. The man's timing was perfect.

"Any suggestions, Molly?" Jonathan inquired, taking a menu.

"The fish is supposed to be good." She lowered her eyes to study her own menu but found she couldn't concentrate on the printed words. Shyly she peeked at Jonathan over the top of her menu. He was completely engrossed, his brows gathered in concentration.

What a wonderful face, she thought, noticing for the first time the way the soft overhead lights played on his striking features. His hair, which had first appeared bright copper, was liberally laced with rich golden highlights. His eyes were a dark aquamarine tinged with flecks of deep blue and were ringed by gloriously long lashes. His face was remarkably smooth, with only a faint shadow of a light beard. His hands, she noted, were large, the fingers well formed and tapered.

Staring at him, Molly was suddenly curious. This was not the type of man who needed to be fixed up with a blind date. While not handsome in the traditional sense, he was good-looking enough. That, coupled with his charming personality and sparkling sense of humor, made him quite appealing. He probably had his pick of women. What on earth was the man doing on a blind date?

"Have you decided yet? Or would you care to study *me* a bit longer?"

Molly's startled gaze flew to his. He had been watching her watch him! She closed her menu and laid it down carefully, pretending to be desperately interested in the delicate pattern of the tablecloth. "No, I've decided."

"And just what have you decided?" he inquired softly as he laid down his own menu. Jonathan's fingers brushed hers, sending a pulse-pounding shiver up her arm. Vividly aware that he wasn't talking about her menu choice, she struggled to maintain a casual air.

"I've decided on the fish," she responded with remarkable calm, startling herself.

"Good. I think I'll have the same." Jonathan signaled the waiter, gave him their order, then sat back while the man poured some wine.

"Now," Jonathan said once they were finally alone, "tell me about yourself."

Molly glanced up at him in surprise. She wasn't used to discussing her personal life with anyone, no matter how handsome or charming. But on the other hand, he was Alma's grandson and she certainly couldn't be rude.

"What would you like to know?"

"Everything. I want to know everything there is to know about Molly Maguire." Jonathan rested his chin in his hand and studied her intently.

Everything? she wondered weakly. She certainly wasn't about to give him a laundry list of her life. Nor was she about to start divulging such personal information as her dress or ring size. Maybe he'd settle for her favorite vegetable. Somehow, she had the feeling that was not the kind of information Jonathan Kent was interested in.

"I—I don't know where to begin," she stammered, nervously fidgeting with her wineglass.

"Well, for starters, do you do this often?"

Molly stared at him blankly. He was off in another direction again. It was almost as hard to keep up with his train of thought as it was to keep up with Aunt Emily's.

"Do what?" She frowned.

"Go out with strange men."

Molly bit back a smile. "No, I think *you're* about the strangest." The moment the words left her mouth, she burst out laughing. Stealing a glance at Jonathan, she was relieved to see him smiling. At least the man could take it as well as he could dish it out. She liked that.

"I guess I deserved that one, didn't I?" he asked warmly, letting his eyes wander over her face.

Molly nodded. "I'm sorry, but I couldn't help it. You walked right into that."

"So I'm about the strangest, huh?" One brow rose menacingly, and he did his best to leer.

"On the contrary." Molly laughed. "Some of my dates have been pretty strange."

"So I've gathered. Tell me about them."

Molly was thoughtful for a moment. This seemed to be a safe subject. At least it was better than talking about herself.

"Well, there was Dwight Eckman. I guess he was about the strangest. Not that he wasn't nice," she added quickly. "It's just that poor Dwight was deathly afraid of women. I spent the entire evening talking to myself. All poor Dwight did was grunt or nod. I have to admit, by the end of the evening I was getting pretty good at interpreting his grunts." Molly smiled at the memory. "Then there was Harold. He chewed tobacco. Spit the vile stuff all over the place. He even challenged me to a spitting contest!" Molly's nose wrinkled, and Jonathan did his best not to smile.

"Did you accept?"

Molly shook her head. "No, I declined. After him there was Spike."

Jonathan's eyes widened. "Spike? Is that a man or a dog?"

Laughing, Molly shook her head. "I'm still not sure. Poor Spike foamed at the mouth and twitched like he had fleas." Jonathan's laughter warmed her, and she realized with a start that she had opened up to him. She was talking to Jonathan as if she had known him for years, not just hours. Odd, she usually took a long time to open up to someone.

"Why on earth do you do it? Why do you go out with them? You're a beautiful, delightful woman. Why do you get roped into these dates?" His voice was so tender that the laughter died on her lips.

Why, indeed? It was an honest question, too bad she couldn't give him an honest answer. What could she tell him? That Paul Host, her former fiancé had hurt and betrayed her? That she no longer had the ability to trust a man? No, she certainly couldn't tell Jonathan Kent that.

"Why do you do it, Jonathan?" she inquired softly, hoping to successfully turn the conversation around. "Why do you go out on blind dates?"

"I don't usually. This is my first night home, and before I even had my bags unpacked, my grandmother was calling the restaurant and making dinner reservations." He smiled crookedly. "Besides, my curiosity was aroused. I couldn't wait to get a look at 'Miss Emily's poor spinster niece.'" His gentle tone took the sting out of his words, but they still hit home.

Hillchester was a small town, and Molly was well aware of what the townfolk thought of her. She had lived here all her life. At twenty-five, she was still single and lived with her maiden aunt and her pet cat. What else were people to think except that she was just a bit strange? It certainly didn't help matters that her aunt kept hauling men home, regardless of their age or infirmity. What no one, including her aunt, realized was that she was perfectly happy,

"So you fell for that 'poor spinster' routine?" she joked, covering her hurt. "It works every time."

Jonathan chuckled softly. "Why do you do it, Molly? Why do you go out on these blind dates?"

So much for turning the conversation around, she thought, flashing him what she hoped was an engaging smile. "Actually, I did it for my aunt."

Jonathan frowned. "Then my date was actually with your aunt?"

"Of course not." Molly shifted uncomfortably. He had a way of deliberately misinterpreting her words. "Your date was with me. But I came for my aunt. She arranged this date...with you...for me." Lord, she was beginning to sound like Aunt Emily again.

"Doesn't your aunt trust you to get your own dates?" Jonathan's brow rose quizzically, and she swallowed nervously.

This was one subject she had hoped to avoid. Yet Jonathan had skillfully turned the conversation around to just this subject. He certainly was a sly one. She'd have to remember that.

Molly looked up at him, and astonishment widened her eyes. The change in his face was subtle, but Molly realized at once, *he knew*. The man knew!

"Your aunt thinks you need a man in your life, right?" He reached across the table and covered her hand with his. Molly's palms began to sweat, and she shifted in her seat. His touch was making her breathing ragged. "What do you think? Do you need a man in your life, Molly?"

Maybe the man didn't grunt or spit like some of her other dates, but he sure had a way of looking at her that made her feel as if she were going down on a roller coaster.

Backed into a corner, Molly shifted her gaze from him. "Men are . . . nice," she admitted with some hesitation.

"I'm glad you think so," he replied, stroking her hand. "But, you still didn't answer my question. Do you need a man in your life?"

Looking at him, Molly realized that the last thing she needed in her life was this particular man. His presence was nearly overwhelming, and his smile was positively lethal.

"I think—" she gulped, then spotted the waiter "—that it's time to eat." The man, bless his heart, hadn't lost his timing. He set their plates down and dutifully refilled their wineglasses. Molly didn't even consider drinking more wine. She was already slightly intoxicated, and not from the wine or any other spirits.

"Molly?" Jonathan leaned across the table, tantalizing her dazed senses with his sweet, masculine scent. "Let me assure you that I neither grunt nor spit. And the only thing I've been known to chew is my food. You're perfectly safe with me." He smiled warmly and Molly began to relax. "However, I do have one slight peccadillo."

Uh, oh, she thought, backing away from him a bit. Here it comes. She knew this man was just too good to be true.

"What's that?" She unconsciously gathered her brows together.

"I have a terrible weakness for beautiful, dark-haired ladies who blush at the drop of a hat and have laughing sapphire eyes." His words stilled everything inside her, and Molly began to wonder just how safe she was with this man. Maybe her other dates hadn't been perfect, but at least she'd known that they were no threat to her fragile heart or starved emotions.

Jonathan Kent, on the other hand, seemed to be a threat to both. Somehow he had managed to captivate and charm her without really trying. His smile and his words seemed to melt some of the ice around her heart. The invisible wall of protection she'd built for herself seemed to crack in the face of those laughing eyes and that gentle smile.

What was it about the man? she wondered as she picked at her food. He was no different from any other man. No, her mind corrected, he was very different. When he looked at her, her mouth felt as if it were full of peanut butter, and her tongue seemed to stick to the roof of her mouth. Her thoughts jumped about with wild abandon, and the most incredible words seemed to fall from her mouth.

Watching him, Molly was amazed. The man even ate elegantly. Did he have to be so darn perfect? It was positively annoying. How on earth was she ever going to get through the rest of the evening, knowing the effect he was having on her?

"Molly? Is something wrong?"

"What?" Jonathan's voice startled her out of her thoughts, and she spoke louder than she intended, causing the couple at the next table to eye her curiously.

"Is everything all right?" Jonathan looked genuinely concerned.

All right? Was the man crazy? Nothing was all right!
"Everything is fine," she lied, taking a bite of fish.
"Just fine." Molly forced herself to concentrate on her
meal, willing her hands to work. Fork to fish, fish to
mouth, chew, swallow, breathe. Her silent instructions
continued until there was nothing left on her plate but
a small piece of lemon.

"I like a woman with a hearty appetite," Jonathan
confided, once the plates were cleared. "Would you like
some dessert?"

"D-dessert?" Molly stuttered. If she had to force her
mouth and teeth to work any more, she'd scream. "No
dessert, thank you. I'm stuffed. Coffee will be fine."

The waiter cleared the table, poured coffee, then
paused to take Jonathan's dessert order.

"Come on, Molly, let's work off our dinner."

"What?" Molly looked up at him. He was standing
next to her, holding out his hand.

"Are you coming? I'm going to look awfully silly out
on the dance floor all by myself." If the smile he flashed
her was meant to be reassuring, it missed its mark. The
idea of having Jonathan's arms around her was more
than her jangled nerves could take at the moment.

"I'm not much of a dancer," she hedged, hoping to
put him off.

"Neither am I," he confessed. "But I've waited all
night for an excuse to hold you in my arms, and I'm not
going to let this opportunity pass."

Before she could protest, Jonathan grabbed her hand,
pulled her from the booth and led her out onto the
dance floor. The song was a soft, slow number, and

Jonathan held her close, his arms wrapped tightly around her.

As he molded her into the protective warmth of his embrace, Molly's senses went into overdrive. Through the thin silk of her dress, she could feel the heat of his hands on her skin. Taking deep, slow breaths, Molly wearily tried to fight back the hypnotic spell that he seemed to weave around her. She struggled to calm her skittering senses, but Jonathan's heady aroma made her dizzy, and she swayed.

"Tired?" Jonathan slid his fingers up to cup the back of her neck, making her skin prickle.

"Yes, a little," she responded, holding herself stiffly.

"Relax, Molly," he whispered softly. "I won't bite."

Biting was not exactly what she was afraid of at the moment. Her usually calm, reasonable mind was failing her, and her emotions were suddenly taking over. Her body was responding to him in a way that made her suddenly conscious of her long-suppressed desires. The heat that emanated from his powerful body seemed to seep into hers. Pore by pore.

Molly's senses were attuned to his reactions, and she realized with a shock that she was having as powerful an effect on him as he was having on her. She could feel the increased tempo of his heart as it beat beneath his shirt and his breath seemed a bit ragged. Did she imagine it, or did his steps seem to falter?

The song ended, and Molly stopped abruptly in the middle of the dance floor, hurriedly pulling herself free from his embrace.

"Hey, where are you going?" he asked. "If we wait a moment, another song will start." That was exactly what she was afraid of! If the band had any heart at all, they would play a polka or an Irish jig—anything so long as she wouldn't have to face going back into the comfort of Jonathan's arms again.

Her ears detected the soft strains of "Moon River," and Molly groaned as Jonathan pulled her into his arms again. With a resigned sigh she leaned against him and buried her face into the soft pad of his shoulder. What could it hurt? It was only a simple dance, for heaven's sake, not a lifelong commitment. Maybe she was just overreacting, she reasoned, as her feet began to move in time with the music.

Deciding it was best to ignore the fact that her body molded perfectly to the contours of his, despite the differences in their height, Molly began to relax.

When Jonathan's hands massaged the small of her back, Molly found to her surprise that she was actually enjoying his touch. She was a grown woman of twenty-five. She certainly couldn't continue to act like a scared jackrabbit simply because this man sent her nerves jumping in a hundred different directions.

Molly closed her eyes as the song played on. Jonathan's shoulder, strong and firm, felt good against her cheek. The soft wool of his suit coat gently stroked her skin, tickling her. When he slipped both his arms around her waist and pulled her closer, she offered no protest, and she slid her arms around his neck, even though she had to stand on her tiptoes to do it. They slowly swayed to the music, their bodies in tune to the tempo.

Her legs grew weak, and she looked up at Jonathan. His eyes were closed, and a small smile played along his mouth. The urge to reach out and caress his lips was so strong that Molly linked her fingers tightly together around his neck, lest she do something foolish. But just for a moment, she wondered what it would feel like to have his mouth on hers. The imagined sensation was so strong that she closed her eyes and forced her mind to go blank.

"Molly?" Jonathan's voice was a husky whisper, and her eyes fluttered slowly open.

"Umm, yes?"

"The song is over."

"Oh!" A pink tinge of embarrassment crept up her face as she snatched her arms free, giving herself a mental shake. She barely knew this man, and she was acting like a lovesick schoolgirl! What on earth was the matter with her? Molly was silent as Jonathan led her off the dance floor and back to their booth.

"More coffee?" Jonathan asked, his voice once again normal.

Molly nodded and deliberately avoided his gaze. Did he have to look at her like that? Didn't he know how much it rattled her? Aware that he was watching her intently, Molly racked her brain for a safe subject to talk about. She certainly didn't want to give him an opportunity to start asking personal questions again.

"How long will you be in town?" she inquired, taking a sip of her coffee.

"I'm not really sure, probably about two weeks. I wish I could stay longer, though—I'm worried about my grandmother." Concern etched his handsome features, and Molly's pulse quickened in alarm.

Her aunt and Jonathan's grandmother, Alma Kent, had been friends for as long as she could remember. Why, Alma Kent, Aunt Emily and Ralph Pritchard did practically everything together. Molly often teased that they were like the three musketeers, because they were always together. The thought that something might be wrong with Alma caused Molly untold concern.

"Is something wrong with your grandmother? Is she ill?" Molly's heart fluttered.

Jonathan shook his head. "No, she's not ill. It's just—well, she's getting on in years and I don't know how much longer she can go on living alone. That house of hers is just too big for her to handle now."

A sudden web of uneasiness wound itself into her thoughts. "What will happen when she can't live alone anymore?" Molly asked casually, absently fingering the rim of her coffee cup. "Will you move her to Portland?"

Jonathan shook his head again. "No, moving my grandmother just wouldn't be practical. I travel a lot and I don't think it's a good idea to uproot her from her friends at this point in her life."

Not practical for who? she wondered. Moving his grandmother to Portland might just cramp his style.

"What will happen to Alma when she can't live alone anymore?" Molly asked again. She was prying, and she knew it, but she was curious to know just what Jonathan Kent's plans for his grandmother were. Alma Kent was like a member of her family, and Molly cared desperately about her.

Jonathan shrugged. "I'm not really sure, Molly. I'm working on a few things for her." He flashed her a charming smile, and Molly stiffened.

I'll just bet you are, she thought sourly. Probably some cold concrete building where his grandmother could idle away her time braiding old rags together or painting happy faces on sleeping turtles.

"What kinds of things?" A ripple of anger rolled up her spine, but she tried not to show it.

To her surprise, Jonathan grinned. "Don't worry, Molly. I assure you my intentions toward my grandmother are completely honorable."

Honorable. A storm cloud began brewing in the depths of Molly's eyes as a sharp pain from the past rose up like bile in her throat. That was exactly the term Paul Host, her former fiancé, had used when he had tried to convince Molly to put Aunt Emily in a home.

Listening to Jonathan talk about his plans for his grandmother, Molly had the most maddening urge to squash his handsome face in the gooey chocolate dessert the waiter had left for him. Like it or not, she realized, she was going to have to keep an eye on him, if only for Alma's sake. If Jonathan Kent thought he was going to waltz in here and—

"Miss Maguire?" The maître d' was at their table, his face a mask of concern. "I don't want to alarm you, but we have an emergency telephone call for you."

"For me?" Molly was too startled to do little more than stare at the man. "Are you sure?" Who on earth knew she was here? Aunt Emily! Her heart began to pound, and the strength seemed to flee from her body.

"Yes, I'm quite sure. If you'll follow me, you can take the call in my office."

Molly rose on trembling legs. Jonathan, sensing her alarm, took control of the situation and put a protective arm around her waist as they hurried through the restaurant.

"Something is wrong. I just know it." Molly clutched Jonathan's sleeve as they entered the office.

"You don't know that yet. Go on, Molly. Answer the phone." He urged her forward.

Molly stared blankly at the telephone for a moment, then lifted the receiver to her ear.

"Hello?" Her voice was a puffy whisper, and her eyes grew wide as she listened attentively.

Watching her face intently, Jonathan stepped closer and put his hands on her shoulders. "Molly?"

Scowling, she shook her head and dropped the receiver. "I don't believe it!"

"Molly? What don't you believe? What's happened?"

Raising her stunned eyes to his, Molly shook her head in disbelief. "Aunt Emily has been arrested!"

Chapter Three

When I get my hands on Clarence Pritchard," Molly muttered as she stormed up the cement stairs of the sheriff's office.

Jonathan caught her arm. "Molly, please, settle down. I'm sure this is just a misunderstanding." She ignored his soothing words and continued up the steps.

"I've known Clarence Pritchard my whole life. He's been known to do some stupid things, but this—" she stopped at the top of the steps and shook her fist "—this has got to take the cake! Arresting Aunt Emily like a common criminal. When I get my hands on him—"She shook free of Jonathan's grasp, yanked the door open and charged inside.

"Where's my aunt?" she demanded, blue eyes blazing.

Junior, the deputy sheriff, calmly sat behind his desk, munching on a hamburger. Spotting Molly, he gallantly wiped a clump of ketchup off his chin and grinned. "Evening, Miss Molly."

Molly glared at him across the counter. "Junior! What the devil is going on around here?"

Junior spotted Jonathan behind her and directed his full attention to the newcomer. "Evening." His grin widened. "New in town, aren't you?" He gave Jonathan a conspiratorial wink. "'Bout time Miss Molly got herself a new beau."

Jonathan dropped a restraining hand on Molly's shoulder just as she began to advance threateningly toward the deputy. She'd wring Junior's neck with her bare hands!

"Good evening, Deputy," Jonathan replied smoothly, tightening his grip on her shoulder. "Yes, as a matter of fact, I am new in town." He extended his hand. "Jonathan Kent."

Junior grinned from ear to ear, then politely wiped his hand on his pants before taking Jonathan's outstretched hand. "Name's Elmer. Most folks around here call me Junior, after my daddy," he added proudly.

Molly rolled her eyes heavenward. These two were idly exchanging pleasantries while her aunt sat in jail!

"Jonathan!" Molly tapped her foot impatiently. "Whose side are you on?"

"Your side," he whispered. "But you're not going to get anywhere in the state you're in. And it's certainly not going to help if you get yourself arrested for disturbing the peace."

"He—" she nodded toward Junior "—he wouldn't dare! I could wrestle him to the ground when we were kids, and I'll do it again if need be." She narrowed her gaze on the blushing deputy. Sensing her displeasure,

Junior shifted uneasily, his eyes darting first to Molly, then to Jonathan.

"Molly, please?" Jonathan groaned, giving her shoulder a little squeeze. "Calm down. Why don't you let me handle this for you? I'm an attorney, remember?"

Molly scowled up at Jonathan. Let him handle it? She wasn't used to letting anyone handle things for her, particularly a man. "Thank you. But I'm quite capable of handling things on my own. Without your help," she added pointedly.

Jonathan stared into her upturned face. "Yes, I'm sure you are," he said smoothly. "But, at the moment, I think you're too upset to see things clearly. Besides, how much experience have you had arranging bail for a prisoner's release?" One brow rose in expectation.

Molly swallowed hard. "P-prisoner's release?" Her stomach lurched helplessly, coming to lodge somewhere in her throat.

Jonathan rocked back on his heels and crossed his arms across his chest. "Yes, release. And how about bail?"

"Bail?" she echoed weakly, lifting her face so that her eyes met his. She'd never even considered Aunt Emily a prisoner. She just assumed she'd come down here, scare the dickens out of Junior and Clarence and then take her aunt home. But release and bail! She didn't have any experience in such matters. Aunt Emily had never gotten herself arrested before.

Molly chewed her lip nervously. Maybe she'd better let Jonathan handle this. Just once, just this one time, she'd have to; under the circumstances she really didn't have much choice.

"Molly?" Jonathan's voice held a question.

"Oh, all right," she snapped, leveling a hostile gaze on Junior again. "You handle it." She stepped back from the counter, keeping a watchful eye on the deputy.

"Pardon me, Junior. Please forgive us for interrupting your evening meal." Jonathan was being deliberately cheerful, and Molly rolled her eyes. This was a small town; most folks hadn't experienced the charms of a big city lawyer before. Judging from poor Junior's reaction, it was going to be quite interesting to watch. "I was wondering if we could trouble you to tell us what the charges are against my client."

"Yes sir." Junior snapped to attention.

Molly rolled her eyes. Charming was one thing, overly solicitous was quite another matter. She gave Jonathan's arm a yank. "Don't apologize to him," she whispered. "He's got a lot of nerve, stuffing his face while my aunt rots in a jail cell." Anger flashed in the depths of her eyes.

Jonathan chuckled softly and shook his head. "Molly, your aunt hasn't even been here an hour yet. I hardly think she's rotting." He gave her a sly wink. "Besides, it doesn't hurt to dazzle the competition," he whispered, causing Molly to stiffen. Was that what Jonathan had been doing to her all evening? Dazzling her? She thought for a moment, then realized that's exactly what Jonathan Kent had been doing to her all evening! The thought only aggravated her more.

Pulling her gaze from Jonathan, Molly stared at Junior. Sensing he was the center of everyone's attention, Junior grabbed his hamburger and continued eating.

"Molly?"

She turned toward Jonathan, and something in his face softened her defenses.

"Trust me, please." Jonathan's voice was caressing, coaxing her into a blurred limbo where time was suspended and all action stopped, except for the pounding of her heart. Trust him? Molly swallowed hard. She hadn't trusted anyone in such a long time. The last person she had trusted was Paul. Look how that turned out.

Surveying Jonathan intently, Molly thought about what he'd said. She didn't even know him, not really. Trust him?

As she stared at him, her nerves flickered awake, then slowly ignited. Something passed between them. It was gone in an instant, leaving her feeling slightly breathless and off kilter.

She'd try, just for now. She'd *try* to trust him. "All right," she finally agreed, wondering about her judgment. "But I want to see my aunt and I don't want to wait until Junior finishes his dinner!" She spun on her heel and headed for the chairs lining the back wall. Molly dropped into a seat, but couldn't sit still. What on earth could her aunt have done? Aunt Emily didn't drive, so it couldn't be parking violations. Nickodemus, their cat, had all his shots. What on earth could the woman have done?

Twisting in her seat, Molly craned her neck, trying to hear the conversation. Jonathan's voice carried across the sparsely furnished room as a well-modulated muffle. Junior's voice was louder, but she could barely make out what he was saying. Even when Junior wasn't eating, she had a hard time understanding the man. Smog had settled in his brain years ago.

Jonathan finally turned and flashed her a thumbs-up sign. Frustrated, Molly jumped up and bounded across the room.

"What's happened? When can I see my aunt? Why was she arrested?" Standing behind Jonathan, she was suddenly struck by how broad his back was. Unconsciously, Molly put her hand on his shoulder, feeling a desperate need to touch him. Jonathan turned, and his gaze collided with hers. His look mesmerized her, and her breath froze in her throat. Frightened by her feelings, Molly yanked her hand back, suddenly feeling foolish.

"I'm sorry," she muttered, cursing the telltale blush she felt creep up her face. "I guess I'm just upset."

Jonathan smiled wickedly. "Don't be sorry, Molly. I understand perfectly. To tell you the truth, I've had a hard time keeping my hands to myself tonight, too." His eyes danced and she squirmed uncomfortably. "But let's wait until we're somewhere more private. Then you can touch me whenever and wherever you want."

"Jonathan!" Molly's face flamed brighter, and she noted that Junior was taking in the entire scene. Lord, the way the gossip mill worked, everyone in town would know about her date with Jonathan by morning. Jamming a rebellious curl back into her braid, Molly struggled for composure. "Please, Jonathan," she whispered hoarsely. "What will Junior think?"

"He'll think Miss Molly's got herself a new beau." Jonathan's boyish grin sent her heart fluttering.

Squaring her shoulders, Molly chose to deliberately ignore Jonathan's words. "What about Aunt Emily? When can I see her?"

"Sheriff Pritchard's on his way back. As soon as he gets here, I'll know more. Seems the deputy doesn't have the faintest idea what's going on." That was nothing new, Molly noted. Junior rarely had any idea what was going on. But, she had to admit, Junior wasn't such a bad guy. Ever since he'd had a crush on her in fourth grade, she'd had a soft spot for him.

Jonathan patted her shoulder. "All we can do is sit and wait." Sitting and waiting was the last thing Molly wanted to do. She paced the office in frantic anticipation. Clarence Pritchard was certainly going to get a piece of her mind.

"Molly, why don't you sit down? You're wearing a hole in the linoleum." Jonathan patted the seat next to him and picked up the evening paper that was lying on the chair. With a deliberate coolness that only increased her agitation, he began working on a crossword puzzle.

When the front door finally opened, Molly sprang at the sheriff, her heart pounding like a jackhammer. "Clarence Pritchard! What the devil is going on around here? I demand to know why you arrested my aunt."

The sheriff tipped his hat politely. "Evening, Miss Molly." Spotting Jonathan, who rose, the sheriff smiled again. "Evening." He glanced back at Molly and gave her a wink. "It's 'bout time you got yourself a new beau," he whispered.

Lord, she thought, here we go again! "Clarence Pritchard, don't you have better things to do with your time than to arrest harmless old women?" Molly stood on tiptoe, hands on her hips, glaring up into the man's jowly face.

"Harmless?" Clarence grunted, then sidestepped Molly. Walking back around the counter, he tossed his hat on the desk. "Your aunt caught me good with that blasted cane of hers." He turned and bent over, pointing delicately to his broad backside.

"Probably deserved it," she muttered under her breath. She felt Jonathan's hand clamp down on her shoulder, and he shot her a warning glance before giving her shoulder a gentle squeeze.

"Molly, please?" Jonathan moaned.

She turned to face him. She had to admire how cool and calm Jonathan appeared. *She* felt as if a powder keg had exploded inside her.

"Sheriff, I'm Jonathan Kent, Miss Maguire's attorney. Would you please tell me what the charges are against my client?"

Molly opened her mouth, but the look Jonathan shot her stopped her, and she clamped her lips closed again. She'd said she'd trust him, she reminded herself darkly.

"Well—" Sheriff Pritchard scratched his chin absently and shook his head "—to start with, there's disturbing the peace. Then there's trespassing." He paused to rub his backside again. "Not to mention assaulting an officer of the court," he added pointedly, giving Molly the full benefit of his hound-dog eyes.

"What the devil are you talking about, Clarence?" Molly's patience with the whole mess was gone, along with her temper.

"Now, Molly, your aunt was picketing again over at the senior center. I asked her to leave. I was real nice 'bout it, too." He shook his head. "You know how stubborn the old gal can be. Your aunt refused to leave."

If he had expected sympathy from her, he was in for a rude awakening. Molly's eyes darkened and she glared up at him. Sensing her displeasure, he rushed on. "Now, Molly, I tried explaining to her that there was nothing I could do 'bout the center being closed down. It's out of my hands. All I can do is try to keep the peace in town, and that means keeping your aunt and the other seniors away from that place."

"Clarence!" Molly's voice was pitched high, and disbelief filled her eyes. "Do you mean to tell me you arrested my aunt because she wouldn't leave the senior center?"

"Yup." He shook his head slowly, then turned his attention to Jonathan. "The center's been closed down, some code violations and things. Owners want to sell the land for a fancy new shopping mall. I hear tell it's gonna be real nice, too. Just what this town needs." Clarence rocked back on his heels, obviously delighted with the idea.

Molly ignored his running commentary. Leave it to Clarence to think a shopping mall would be a grand idea. He'd probably welcome the plague, too.

"You could have done something, Clarence! Anything! But you didn't have to arrest her!" Shock clipped Molly's words, and her breath came in short, jerky gasps.

"What's Miss Emily's bail, sheriff?" Jonathan was the epitome of staid, calm composure.

The sheriff scratched himself again and shifted nervously. "Seeing's how I've known Miss Emily all my life, I'll go easy on her." He thought for a moment and then flashed them a toothy grin. "Two hundred dollars."

"What!" Molly lunged across the counter at him, determined to do bodily harm if she got her hands on him. Jonathan caught her around the waist and lifted her off the floor before she reached the sheriff.

"Clarence Pritchard!" she screeched over her shoulder. "Aunt Emily's right about you. You didn't have a lick of sense when you were a child, and I can't say that I've seen any improvement in the years since!"

Carrying her across the room, Jonathan deposited
her on the nearest empty chair and shook his head.
"Molly Maguire, don't you dare move from this chair
until I tell you to! At this rate, I'll have to wire Portland for bail money for the whole lot of us." Jonathan's jaw twitched, and he glared down at her. "One
more thing: be quiet until I'm finished." With that, he
spun on his heel.

She angrily slid back against the wall and clenched
her fists. Was Clarence out of his mind? Where on earth
was she supposed to get that kind of money this late at
night? She was a school teacher, not a banker!

Fuming, Molly watched as Jonathan counted out a
stack of bills and handed them to the sheriff. A few
moments later Jonathan approached her, a wide smile
on his face. "The fine is paid, Molly. Your aunt is free."

Relief flooded her, and Molly jumped from the chair,
ran across the room, and threw her arms around his
neck. "Jonathan, thank you! I don't know what I
would have done without you," she gushed. "How can
I ever repay you?"

"I'm sure we can think of something," Jonathan
whispered, hugging her tight. "I'm sure we can think of
something."

His nearness made Molly's legs tremble. Finally
Jonathan released her and held her at arm's length. For
a long moment they stared at each other in silence.
Molly was vaguely aware that something deep inside of
her was slowly fluttering awake. Her heart raced and her
pulse danced. Jonathan's eyes seemed to stroke her
more gently than a caress, and Molly shivered. The dull,
stuffy air of the sheriff's office suddenly seemed elec-
trified.

"Come on, Molly," Jonathan said softly, breaking the spell. "Let's go find someplace quiet to wait."

Feeling oddly uncomfortable, Molly deliberately avoided Jonathan's gaze as she followed him to the chairs at the back of the room. Her tongue seemed to have deserted her in her hour of need, and she couldn't think of one intelligent thing to say, so she sat down and remained silent.

A few moments later Sheriff Pritchard dutifully helped her aunt into the room. Molly wasn't too surprised to see Clarence holding her aunt's cane carefully out of the woman's reach. Good thing, too, Molly thought with a trace of humor. Molly knew that when her aunt found out the size of her bail, she was likely to use her cane on poor Clarence again.

"Aunt Emily! Are you all right?" Molly rushed to her and folded the small woman into her arms.

"All right?" Aunt Emily frowned. "Why, of course, I'm all right, dear. Why wouldn't I be?" She looked at Molly as if she was behaving like an addle-brained child.

"Why, indeed?" Molly chuckled softly, then hugged her aunt tight. "Come on, let's go home."

"Clarence!" Aunt Emily's voice rang loud with indignation, capturing the sheriff's attention. "I do believe you have something that belongs to me." She nodded toward her cane, but Clarence shook his head.

"I'll give this back to you, Miss Emily, but only if you promise not to go around hitting people with it." He grimaced and rubbed his backside gingerly. "This thing is dangerous."

"Nonsense!" Emily snatched the cane from Clarence, causing him to jump back out of her reach. "And don't think I'm not going to mention this to your father, young man." She pointed her cane in his direction again, and Clarence hung his head sheepishly.

"Ah, Miss Emily," he whined. "I was just doing my job."

"Humph! We'll see about your job come election time. Just might decide to run for sheriff myself!" She studied him coolly. Finally, satisfied that he had gotten her point, she turned to Molly. As she spotted Jonathan for the first time, Emily's face brightened, and she smiled girlishly. "Jonathan, dear," she crooned, "it's nice to see you again. Now I know the reason for my niece's glowing face."

"Aunt Emily!" Molly blushed to her ears. Leave it to her aunt to say exactly what was on her mind!

"Ladies, I think our business here is concluded." Jonathan gallantly held out an arm for each of them and led them out of the sheriff's office.

In the car, Aunt Emily chatted away as if nothing out of the ordinary had happened, without giving Molly a chance to question her about her latest escapade. It wasn't until they were inside the house that Emily dropped yet another bombshell.

"Jonathan, dear, since you're an attorney, would you mind looking into the problem at the senior center? They've closed the place down because of some code violations or some such nonsense. Ridiculous if you ask me." She smiled sweetly and patted Jonathan's arm. "It sure would mean a lot to me. The senior center is the only place we can meet and socialize with people our own age. It's been part of this town for as long as I can remember. Whatever the problem, I'm sure you can take care of it for us, dear." Emily faked a pain-filled sigh that didn't fool Molly for a moment. She knew the twinkle in her aunt's eyes very well. But Jonathan seemed completely taken in. Her aunt sure hadn't lost her touch, Molly thought, smothering a chuckle. It was time for her to put a stop to her aunt's shenanigans. Poor Jonathan didn't stand a chance.

"Aunt Emily," Molly said firmly. "Jonathan is only going to be here for a short time. I doubt that he'll be able to do anything to help. Besides, I'm sure he has other things planned for his vacation." She met Jonathan's gaze over the top of her aunt's head, and he gave her a wink.

"Nonsense!" Emily snapped, turning to give Molly the full benefit of her blue eyes. "I'm sure Jonathan can help us. And you can help him." Emily smiled sweetly and Molly cringed. That smile was a sure sign of trouble.

"Miss Emily, I'll be glad to do anything I can to help," Jonathan offered with a smile. He gave Molly a helpless shrug.

Emily fairly beamed. "Wonderful, dear. I knew we could count on you."

"Oh, dear, it's been such a trying evening, would you mind helping me off with my coat?" Emily patted the area near her heart and gave Jonathan her full attention as he politely helped her remove her coat.

Molly realized her aunt had done it again. Whenever Aunt Emily didn't want to discuss something, she abruptly changed the subject. But this time, it wasn't going to work.

"Aunt Emily—" Molly stopped as a round of sneezes rocked Jonathan.

"Catching cold, dear?" Emily inquired sweetly, giving Jonathan's arm a reassuring pat. "You'd better take care of yourself."

Jonathan rubbed his eyes. "I don't think it's a cold. I think I'm just allergic to the fur on your coat."

Emily yanked the offending article from his arms and promptly hung it in the closet. "Can't have you sick now, Jonathan. We need you."

Molly rolled her eyes and sighed. Her aunt was laying it on rather thick, even for her.

"Well, children, I think I'll say good-night." Emily sniffed delicately, and Molly bit her bottom lip to keep from chuckling.

"Jonathan, you're in trouble now," Molly teased after her aunt had gone. "Once Aunt Emily trusts you, you have a friend for life."

Jonathan leaned his weight against the front door and dimmed the foyer light, bathing the room in a shadowy haze. "How about you, Molly? Do you trust me? Are you my friend?" His voice had dropped to a whisper and Molly shivered. The conversation had taken a sudden and unexpected turn, and she wasn't at all certain she liked where it was going.

"Of course, I'm your friend," she returned softly, taking a step back. She needed to put some distance between them in order to think. For some reason, the closer Jonathan got, the harder it was for her brain to function.

"What if I want more than a friend, Molly?" He reached out and caught her hand in his. His nearness was making her heart pound. "You never answered my question, either." Her pulse fluttered as he slowly drew her hand upward. She was shocked by the velvet softness of his mouth as he pressed his lips to her open palm.

"Wh-what question?" she managed to get out. His eyes locked on hers, and his warm breath sent a tingling feeling through her as his lips gently teased her willing hand.

"Do you need a man in your life, Molly?" His thumb moved gently to caress her wrist with feather strokes. She caught her breath as his fingers slowly traced a delicate little pattern, working their way slowly up her arm until a wave of intoxicating shivers raced through her. "You're shivering," he whispered. His voice was as tender as a spring breeze. "Does my touch bother you?"

"N-no," she fibbed, blinking rapidly. "I'm just ticklish." She tried to force some order into her distracted thoughts as his fingers continued their journey, slowly skipping up her arm. Even through the thin silk of her sleeves, his touch burned. His warm fingers cupped her neck, tenderly caressing the bare skin, which only increased the lethargy that made her legs tremble and scrambled her common sense.

"Your hair feels like silk," he whispered, slowly undoing the neatly braided plait. His fingers combed through the heavy strands of her hair, and Molly had to force her lungs to work. Why hadn't she noticed the thickly corded muscles of his neck? Or the way his voice deepened when he spoke her name? Or the way his lips seemed so warm, so inviting?

"Come here, Molly." The words seemed to echo from deep within the wall of his chest, and Molly took a deep breath. Jonathan was so close that the masculine scent of him filled her senses, heating the blood in her veins to the boiling point. "Molly, come here," he repeated, trailing his fingers down the silky strands of her hair to the pulse points of her throat. Pushing back her loose hair, he bent his head to nuzzle her neck.

Her heart thumped, and Molly feared he could see its increased tempo through the thin material of her dress. She struggled to regain some control of her senses, which were reacting to him in a way that confused her.

"Don't be afraid of me, Molly." He flashed her a wide smile, then slid his other arm around her narrow waist, pulling her so close that she could feel his heart beating.

Her dark lashes fluttered nervously. That smile, she thought, could charm a grizzly bear with a toothache. She watched in a trance as his mouth hovered close to hers. Unconsciously she licked her lips, which suddenly felt parched. Molly tried to ignore the fingers that skipped along her spine, but a sweet flow of momentary weakness seeped into her pulsing veins, and it took all of her self-control not to sag limply against Jonathan's broad chest.

Jonathan's mouth, warm and moist, trailed across her temples. Emotions long dormant began to stir, frightening her.

"Jonathan, wait," she protested, lifting a hand to his chest. "I don't think—"

"Don't think, Molly," he murmured, ignoring her hand, "just feel." His lips trailed down her cheek to nuzzle the soft patch of tender skin along her jawline.

"But, Aunt Emily..." Her words faltered as he lowered his lips to tease the curve of her mouth.

"Sorry, Molly," he whispered against her skin. "Your aunt will have to get her own man." His mouth dropped again to tease the corners of her lips, and Molly shuddered as a torrent of conflicting emotions tore through her, adding to her confusion.

Anticipation ached through her weary limbs. If he was going to kiss her, she wished he'd hurry up. He was driving her crazy!

"Molly," he moaned. "You taste so good." His breath was sweet, and she arched closer to him, anxious for his touch. Apprehension and desire mingled in a blur as his lips teased hers. Her breath withered as he gently seduced her mouth. "Now, Molly?"

She wound her arms tightly around his neck and sighed. "Now, Jonathan."

His parted lips met hers, shocking her. He tasted sweeter than she'd ever expected. Molly tightened her arms around him, rocked by the tide of desire that flowed through her. Jonathan slowly pulled his mouth from hers, and Molly's lids fluttered open in surprise. "Is that it?"

Jonathan gazed at her for a moment, then chuckled softly. "No, Molly, that's just the beginning." His mouth came down on hers again, this time with more urgency. She leaned into him, forgetting everything but the wonderful strong feel of his arms around her and the wonderful taste of his lips, soft and tender, on hers.

Molly's breath lodged in her throat as his hands tightened around her waist. Shivers of desire danced through her. She savored the taste of him, reveling in his embrace. His mouth worked slowly over hers, yet with an intensity that could not be ignored. Lost in a tidal wave of emotions, Molly refused to heed the voice of protest that rudely hammered at her foggy brain.

Suddenly Jonathan pulled back, a strange look on his face. Startled by his abruptness, which left her reeling and feeling foolish, Molly stared at Jonathan. His eyes were red and swollen.

"Jonathan, what's wrong?"

"You don't have a cat, do you?" he gasped, his eyes wide.

Oh, Lord, Nickodemus. "Y-yes," she stammered helplessly as she turned up the light.

"I'm severely allergic to cats—to anything with fur, particularly living things." He snatched a snowy white handkerchief from his back pocket as a round of sneezes rocked him. Jonathan edged toward the door, the handkerchief over his face. "I have to get out of here, Molly, I can't breathe."

She nodded, then unlocked the door and yanked it open. Jonathan lunged outside, still holding the handkerchief over his face.

"Shut the door!" he commanded. Molly did as she was told, scanning the room for the offending cat.

"Molly?" Jonathan whispered through the door. "Are you there?"

She pressed her hand against the door where she thought his face might be. "I'm here."

"I had a wonderful time, Molly. I must admit it was a very strange first date, but I did enjoy it." The humor was back in his voice, and she could almost see his smile.

"Thank you," she whispered back. "So did I." She touched her fingers to her lips and felt a sudden thrill as she remembered his lips on hers. "I'm sorry about the cat. And thank you for helping my aunt."

"You're welcome, and don't worry about the cat. I'll be fine in a few minutes." After a long pause, he said, "Molly?"

"Yes?"

"Can I see you tomorrow? Maybe we can have a picnic supper."

Molly smiled and leaned against the door. "Sure, a picnic sounds nice."

"I'd better pick you up out in front, just in case. All right?"

She could hear him reeling with another round of sneezes, and her heart melted. "That's fine, Jonathan. I'll handle the food. Is seven all right?"

"Seven is fine. Good night, Molly," he whispered tenderly.

"Good night, Jonathan," she whispered back, touching the door again.

"Oh, Molly? You never answered my question." There was another long pause, and then he said, "Tomorrow's another day."

Molly smiled in spite of herself. "Good night, Jonathan," she said firmly as she listened to his footsteps echo down the hall. Sighing happily, she leaned against the door.

Suddenly she bolted upright, a look of fear on her face. Good Lord, what on earth had she done?

Chapter Four

Pssst. Molly?" Emily's hushed whisper came through the darkness, snapping Molly out of her reverie.

"Yes, Aunt Emily?" She hoped her voice sounded more normal than she felt. Self-consciously she straightened her mussed hair and snapped on the light before crossing to the living room.

"Is Jonathan gone already, dear?" Emily peeked around her bedroom door.

"You can stop your whispering." Molly laughed. "He's gone." It was her long-standing habit to sit and chat with her aunt after a date. They had been doing it since Molly had begun dating back in high school.

Emily entered the room at a trot, pink foam curlers flying and a mischievous smile on her face. The tips of her fluffy purple slippers peeked out from beneath her red flannel nightgown. "How'd it go, dear?" Though her aunt's voice was calm, Molly could sense her excitement.

"It went . . . well," she admitted reluctantly.

"Wonderful. Alma said Jonathan was a dear boy." Emily smiled happily. Molly knew that smile all too well.

"Now, Aunt Emily," Molly said carefully, tempering her words, "it was just a simple date. Nothing more. Nothing less." There was no sense in Aunt Emily getting her hopes up. Molly didn't want her aunt to have any illusions about her and Jonathan. A faint smile curved her lips, and Molly suddenly wished *she* felt the conviction of her words.

"Nonsense! Sit down and tell me about it." Emily moved to the couch and sat down. Patting the cushion next to her, she looked up expectantly.

Molly sighed. Kicking off her shoes, she curled up next to her aunt. "There's really not much to tell," she hedged, then frowned. "Aunt Emily, we have a few other matters to discuss besides my date with Jonathan Kent." She raised an eyebrow and cocked her head. "Like how you got yourself arrested tonight. What on earth happened? And what were you doing at the senior center so late at night?"

Smiling at the look on Molly's face, Emily dismissed Molly's questions with an airy wave of her hand. "You know Clarence. Gets carried away with himself. Not to worry, dear. The matter's all taken care of." Emily's smile brightened and Molly cringed.

"What's taken care of?" Molly asked.

Emily frowned. "Jonathan didn't stay very long, dear, how come?"

Molly stirred uneasily. Her aunt was doing it again, changing the subject in midstream. But she knew that until she told Aunt Emily all about her date with Jonathan, there was no hope of getting any information

about her aunt's latest escapade. Sighing, Molly shook
her head. Might as well get it over with. Not that she
minded. They'd had some wonderful times in the past,
laughing and talking about some of Molly's dates. And
Molly had to admit that some of those dates had been
pretty laughable.

Tucking her legs under her, Molly leaned back on the
couch. "It seems that Jonathan is allergic to Nickodemus." Remembering Jonathan's hasty exit brought a
smile to her face.

"Glad to hear it," Emily chortled. "Maybe now
you'll get rid of that blasted animal."

"Aunt Emily!" Molly tried to look shocked. "I have
absolutely no intention of getting rid of Nickodemus.
You know how I feel about him." Emily made a face
that left little doubt as to how she felt about the animal. But, no matter how much her aunt protested,
Molly knew her real feelings. It was her aunt who had
brought the stray home. Molly had been about ten years
old at the time. Nickodemus had been hurt. The poor
little thing had been scared and terribly malnourished.
Her aunt had lovingly nursed the wounded stray back
to health, all the time insisting that once the cat was
well, she was going to send him on his way. But, by the
time Nickodemus was well, he was firmly entrenched in
their household, and he and Molly were inseparable.
Even though her aunt enjoyed complaining about
Nickodemus, Molly knew she loved him, too.

"This one's a nice one, dear."

Molly ignored her aunt's wistful tone and blinked
sleepily. "Nickodemus?" she teased.

Emily patted her arm encouragingly. "Jonathan,
dear. Nice looking, too. Not like some of the others.
Remember Roger?" She chuckled softly. "Wasn't he

the one that wore a Christmas ornament around his neck?''

Molly laughed at the memory and nodded her head. ''That's the one. And it wasn't a Christmas ornament, Aunt Emily. It was a gold medallion.'' Roger was into gold chains in a big way. One in particular had caught her aunt's eye. It was a large, intricately designed medallion of his zodiac sign that hung all the way down to the middle of Roger's chest. The man had so many chains wound around his neck, Molly couldn't understand how he stayed upright. The weight alone should have toppled him.

''Didn't notice any ornaments around Jonathan's neck, dear,'' Emily observed cheerfully, and Molly couldn't help it: she smiled. Jonathan was definitely not the ornament type.

''No,'' she admitted, suddenly remembering the way her arms felt wrapped around Jonathan's neck. A shiver raced through her, and she tried to banish the memory from her mind. ''He . . . he doesn't seem to wear any ornaments.''

''Smells nice, too.''

Molly laid her head back against the couch. She certainly couldn't argue with her aunt about that. Jonathan Kent did smell good. Wonderful, in fact. She closed her lids dreamily, and Jonathan's face came into view. The sound of his voice echoed in her mind, and the scent of him engulfed her. Yes, Jonathan Kent smelled good. Too good. It made her nervous.

Molly nodded slowly. ''Yes, he smells good, too.''

Emily's smile brightened a notch. ''Seems to be able to walk unassisted, too.''

Molly nodded again. And waited. She had a feeling her aunt was leading up to something, in a roundabout way, of course, but definitely up to something. Molly wasn't quite sure where the conversation was heading. She never was with her aunt.

Emily's eyes grew dreamy. "Noticed he doesn't have a hairy mouth, either."

Molly bit her lip to keep from laughing. Aunt Emily didn't take kindly to the idea of men with mustaches. "No, Aunt Emily, Jonathan doesn't have a hairy mouth, either." What he had, she thought wistfully, was the softest mouth she had ever kissed. And the sweetest. Molly's lids closed as her senses took over. When Jonathan had lowered his lips toward hers, a pulsating fever had shot through her limbs, leaving her weak and breathless with anticipation. When his mouth had finally captured hers, she had given in completely to the feelings that rolled through her, without regard for the consequences. In that instant, when Jonathan's mouth had touched hers, he had jolted her senses in a way that frightened her. Her reactions to him were startling.

A wave of longing washed over Molly as she replayed the scene in her mind: the way the muscles of his broad back felt beneath her fingers, the way his body fit perfectly to hers, the way his hands wrapped securely around her waist. Desire seemed to burn a path through her, frazzling her nerve endings.

"Molly?" Her aunt's voice startled her, and Molly's eyes flew open in surprise. Her aunt smiled knowingly, bringing a heated flush to Molly's face.

Recovering quickly, Molly faked a yawn and stretched. "I'm really tired," she fibbed rather unconvincingly. "I almost nodded off there for a moment."

Amusement danced in Emily's eyes, and Molly knew she hadn't fooled her for a moment. "He's real helpful, too," Emily continued. "Look at the way he came to my rescue this evening."

"Yes," Molly admitted a bit grudgingly, well aware that her aunt was probably getting ready to zero in for the kill. "He's helpful, too."

"Alma was right. Jonathan is a good boy." Emily measured Molly with her eyes, as if waiting for her to agree. When Molly didn't respond, Emily continued. "Sure don't find many like him anymore."

Ahhh, Molly thought, so this was what her aunt was leading up to. Emily wanted to be absolutely certain Molly was aware that she had finally found a "good one."

A sparkle of annoyance made Molly tense. At the moment she wasn't sure she wanted to hear any more about Jonathan Kent or his virtues. As it was, Molly was having a hard enough time chasing the man from her mind. And she really didn't need her aunt reminding her just how wonderful Jonathan was. Molly was trying to forget!

Satisfied that Molly had gotten her message, Emily smiled once more. "Gonna see him again?" she prompted hopefully.

Molly's sense of humor took over. Even though her aunt had been less than subtle, Molly didn't have the heart to be upset with her. She knew her aunt only wanted her to be happy. Why else would she have devoted most of her time these past few years to hauling home men who had hairy lips, men who wore Christmas ornaments around their necks, and even some men who were old enough to be Aunt Emily's dates—hoping to find a good one among the assortment?

For just a moment, Molly contemplated telling her aunt not to get her hopes up about Jonathan Kent, but she quickly dismissed the idea. Her aunt probably wouldn't pay any attention to her, anyway. Jonathan Kent was not about to become a permanent fixture in Molly's life. She wasn't in the market for a man. Good or otherwise. Her aunt had never listened to her before; no doubt she wouldn't listen now.

"Well?" Emily was waiting in anxious anticipation.

"Yes, Aunt Emily," she finally admitted with a laugh, "I'm going to see Jonathan again. We're going on a picnic tomorrow. But don't—"

Her aunt jumped from the couch. "Then you'd better get to bed, dear. We've got to get up early. There's chicken to fry and pies to bake. I'll bet Jonathan likes apple pie. I'll slice the apples myself in the morning." Emily frowned and patted her lip with a finger in concentration. "Maybe I should get started now."

Molly shook her head in amazement at her aunt's sudden burst of energy. "Aunt Emily, Jonathan's not picking me up until seven. We'll have plenty of time. And it's not necessary to go to all that trouble. We can just have sandwiches."

"Sandwiches!" The word came out like a shot, and Molly had the feeling she had just announced she was going to serve Jonathan fried ants.

"Yes, sandwiches. Aunt Emily, we're going on a picnic. This is not the feast of—"

"Nonsense! Some brie cheese and a nice light wine, too," her aunt continued, totally ignoring Molly's protests. "You'd better get to bed now, dear. It's late and you need your beauty sleep." She smiled mischievously. "Wouldn't want you to look tired for your date with Jonathan."

With a resigned sigh, Molly bent to pick up her shoes. If she hoped to forget about the man, she wasn't going to get the chance with her aunt around. She suddenly bolted upright. Her aunt had almost done it again! "Aunt Emily," she said firmly. "You never did tell me what happened at the senior center tonight. What on earth were you doing there?" Her words were said to her aunt's retreating back. As if sensing she was about to have to answer some questions, Emily had already started padding toward her bedroom.

"Aunt Emily?"

"Not to worry, dear," Emily said breezily, before shutting her bedroom door. "I told you, the matter's taken care of."

Outwitted again, Molly thought with a trace of humor. One of these days she was actually going to pin her aunt down and force her to give a straight answer. Molly smiled. Wishful thinking. Her aunt was as slippery as a snake when it came to something she didn't want to discuss. And right now she didn't want to discuss the senior center. Or her arrest. All she wanted to discuss was Jonathan Kent.

Emily opened her door a crack. "Besides, Jonathan said he'd help us with the matter. He's a good boy, Molly." With a wide smile, Emily promptly closed her door again.

Jonathan Kent again! Molly marched to her room. The man seemed able to do quite a lot of things well, Molly thought with just a touch of resentment. Including winning her aunt over, which was no small feat.

Molly's eyes narrowed as she yanked off her dress and dropped it to the floor. All in all, she decided, she'd heard just about enough about Jonathan Kent and his virtues for one night.

She pulled on her nightgown and snapped off the light. She was going to bed, and she simply was not going to think about him anymore. She fully intended to get a good night's sleep, and not because she needed her beauty sleep, either, but because she was tired. Period.

Molly slid into bed, rolled over and tucked the covers up under her chin. She closed her eyes, and a vision of a laughing, redheaded giant filled her thoughts. Punching her pillow in annoyance, she turned over, squeezed her eyes tightly shut and, with a determined effort, began to count sheep.

Molly was almost asleep before she realized that each and every one of the curly haired little creatures appeared to be a redhead!

"Don't you think you should be getting ready for your date with Jonathan, dear? It's almost five."

Molly's eyes narrowed. It wasn't enough that the man had darkened her dreams and haunted her night so that she'd hardly had a wink of peaceful sleep, but, much to her chagrin, he had even managed to dog her thoughts for nearly every moment of this new day.

A soft, exasperated sigh slipped Molly's pursed lips, and she wiped her hands vigorously on her apron. No sense taking out her annoyance on Aunt Emily. It certainly wasn't her fault that Jonathan Kent had managed to nestle deep in the recesses of Molly's mind.

"Maybe you're right, Aunt Emily. I probably should start getting ready. I'll finish packing up this food after I take my shower." Pushing a tumble of dark hair from her forehead, Molly grabbed the bowl of potato salad she had been mixing and snapped the plastic lid on before depositing it in the refrigerator.

"Why don't you wear that lovely yellow sundress, dear?" Emily suggested helpfully, and Molly scowled.

"Aunt Emily," she began with forced patience. "I hardly think a ruffled yellow sundress is right for a picnic in the park. I'm wearing a pair of jeans and a shirt," she announced firmly, not wishing to put any more emphasis on the date than necessary.

It was just a simple picnic date, she reminded herself as she pulled off her apron and stalked to her room. Just because Jonathan had occupied her thoughts all morning was no reason to treat this date—or this man— any different from any of the other dates she'd had in recent memory.

With firm determination, Molly strode to her closet and picked out a pair of soft, worn jeans and a white cotton shirt. She examined the jeans carefully. They were old and worn and extremely comfortable. She frowned. They also looked as if they'd been through several wars. Maybe she should wear her new jeans. Not for any reason, she assured herself, except that she did need to break them in. She searched her closet until she found the new pants and quickly snapped them from the hanger. She dismissively tossed them onto the bed and headed for the shower.

The hot water helped to ease some of the weariness from her body. She hadn't had such a restless night in ages. Not since she had broken up with Paul.

Thoughts of her former fiancé brought a flood of memories to her mind and even the heat of the water couldn't prevent a convulsive shiver skipping up her spine. The pain was still raw, the wound still deep. How could she have forgotten so quickly?

Paul Host had seemed warm and charming at first, but then— A sharp stab of pain hit Molly and she closed her eyes.

One night shortly before their wedding Paul had called to tell her he had a wonderful surprise for her. She remembered how touched she had been. Paul Host was not the type of man to go in for anything as frivolous as surprises. Delighted with the sudden and unexpected change in him, Molly had happily talked a blue streak that night as Paul had guided his compact car out of town. When he pulled to a stop in front of a large gray concrete building several miles outside of town, Molly was puzzled. She looked at the building carefully, This was her surprise? Not wanting to spoil Paul's obvious delight, she remained silent and just a bit confused.

When Paul had helped her from the car, he'd kept a protective arm around her shoulder, which was something else that she had found unusual. Paul didn't believe in public shows of affection. Conservative to the core, he had never so much as held her hand in public. And in private, he hadn't done much more.

"This is it, darling," Paul crooned proudly, urging her forward. "Isn't it wonderful? I've been searching for just the right place for months." His face was animated and he was beaming from ear to ear.

"Paul, what are we doing here? What is this place?" Molly stared in confusion at the building and the surrounding grounds. The place was well kept, with perfectly manicured lawns and a large garden dotted with fragrant blooms. Keeping a smile firmly planted on her face, she turned to Paul. His obvious excitement was making her just a tad nervous. Paul was not given to bouts of excitement. This abrupt change in his personality was very strange and a bit unnerving.

"It's really quite perfect, don't you think?" he repeated, ignoring her questions. "My attorneys have assured me that this place is quite reputable." He nodded his head vigorously. "It has their full stamp of approval."

Paul seemed to be deliberately avoiding her questions and Molly's heart beat a little faster. She touched his arm gently. "Paul, yes, it's quite nice. But, what does Sunnydale Acres have to do with us?"

His thin lips curved upward in a jubilant smile. "Darling, it's Aunt Emily's new home! Isn't it wonderful?" He hugged her tight. "I want you to know this is one of the most expensive rest homes in the county," he proclaimed proudly, "but, nothing is too good for *our* Aunt Emily." He was positively beaming, and Molly's heart skipped frantically.

Rest home? Molly turned to stare at him in shocked disbelief. Maybe Paul was the one that needed a rest. He expected her aunt to live here? In a rest home? Molly looked at the cold, forbidding building, and a convulsive shudder raced through her. This had to be a terrible mistake. Maybe she had simply misunderstood Paul.

Molly shook her head, trying to clear the turbulance that rocked her frame. "Paul," she began gently, "I don't understand. I thought we agreed that Aunt Emily would live with us after we were married. We discussed it, remember? The night you asked me to marry you. We both agreed that Aunt Emily could continue to make her home with us." She stared at him hopefully, but the look on his face caused her spirits to nosedive.

"I know, Molly, but this place is wonderful. Clean, well managed, close to Hillchester. What more could we want?"

"But Paul—"

"Darling, this will be much better for all of us." Paul dropped his voice to a slow, well-modulated tone, as if he were talking to a petulant child. "Molly, here your aunt will have friends her own age, people with common interests."

She struggled to hold on to her composure.

"And," he went on, nuzzling her neck, "maybe *we* can finally have some privacy."

Her frown quickly deepened to a scowl. Privacy? They'd had all the privacy they'd wanted. Aunt Emily never interfered in their relationship, and she was always careful to give her and Paul plenty of time alone. Not that they'd needed it. Other than a few impassioned kisses, they had never done anything in private that they couldn't do in public. Or in front of Aunt Emily. So what the devil was he talking about?

"Paul, I'm afraid I don't understand. What about Aunt Emily's house? You know there's room for all of us." Her eyes slid back to the building and a sense of foreboding engulfed her. "I couldn't bear to put my aunt away in this place," she whispered hoarsely.

"Darling, you're not putting her away, simply relocating her someplace where she'd be more comfortable." His voice had taken on a soothing tone, but Molly wasn't soothed; she was furious.

Paul had to be insane, not to mention incredibly insensitive. How could he even think about making a decision like this without even bothering to consult her about it?

"It's out of the question, Paul," she stated firmly, stepping out of his embrace. "You've known from the beginning of our relationship that my aunt was a big part of my life. She's the only family I have left. I can't stand the thought of putting her away somewhere. Her home is with us, with people who love her." She hated the pleading tone her voice had taken on, but she had never expected something like this.

"You're not putting her away," Paul argued firmly, his lips curved in a stubborn, tight-lipped smile. "Think of this as . . . as an opportunity to finally live your own life. I understand how you might feel an odd sense of duty and responsibility to the old woman—"

"Paul!" Her voice had been sharp with shock. "Aunt Emily is not an old woman, and I won't have you talking about her like that. I love her, and it doesn't have anything to do with duty or responsibility. I *want* her to be part of our lives."

"Well, I don't." He pouted. "You don't need her anymore. I'll take care of you now." He sounded like a little boy trying to coax a younger child into giving him a piece of candy. Molly looked at him with fresh eyes and, for the first time, saw him as he really was.

"Paul," she snapped, losing her last bit of self-control, "I don't need you to take care of me. I can take care of myself!"

"Molly—" an exasperated sigh lifted his slender shoulders "—I've tried to be patient and reasonable. Now I think it's about time for you to be reasonable, too. I thought you'd appreciate the fact that I'm willing to bear the cost of the woman's upkeep. I can't begin to tell you how expensive a place like this is. But I'm willing to make the sacrifice. The least you can do is be appreciative." He was pouting again, and Molly's temper erupted.

Sacrifice? Upkeep? He was talking about her aunt as if she were a pet to be shipped off and boarded in some kennel to await her everlasting rest! Molly looked at the man she had promised to spend the rest of her life with. Now she realized she couldn't stand to spend another

moment with him, let alone the rest of her life. How
could she have so misjudged him? How could she have
been so blind?

"Molly? Did you hear me? I'm afraid I'm going to
have to insist on these arrangements. You'll have to
make a choice. Either your aunt moves here or I'll have
to seriously reconsider my marriage proposal." It was
an outright threat and the last straw.

Molly's temper boiled over. Why on earth was she
standing here arguing with this heartless, inconsiderate
nincompoop? She yanked his engagement ring off her
finger and thrust it into his hand. "Paul," she said with
exaggerated sweetness, "shove it!"

Molly had decided right then and there that she
would never allow another man to get close enough to
hurt her. Or her aunt. She didn't need or want a man in
her life if it meant sacrificing someone she loved. If a
man didn't have enough love in his heart for her *and*
Aunt Emily, well, then she didn't need the man.

Not even if he had laughing eyes. Molly scowled and
thrust her head under the now-cool water. Jonathan
Kent had sneaked back into her thoughts again. He had
caught her off guard the night before. The man had
charged into her life with all the subtlety of a high-speed
freight train, intoxicating her with his smile, dazzling
her with his charm and melting the icy wall around her
heart with his fiery kisses.

Shaking the water from her hair, Molly stepped from
the shower. Lord, what on earth did the man do for an
encore?

Grabbing a towel, she vigorously rubbed her wet
head. All day long she had thought about breaking their
date. But what could she possibly say? What reason
could she give? "I'm sorry, Jonathan, but I can't pos-

sibly see you anymore because I'm terribly attracted to you?'' That he had a way of looking at her that made her pulse dance to its own private beat? Molly moaned in disgust. She certainly wasn't about to tell him that, even if it was the blasted truth.

Last night was supposed to be just another boring date with an equally boring man. Jonathan Kent was about as boring as the Fourth of July. And that smile of his! He ought to register it as a lethal weapon, she thought dismally.

Just look at the way he had charmed her aunt! All day long she'd had to listen to her aunt's glowing words of appreciation about the man. Molly couldn't have stopped thinking about Jonathan even if she'd wanted to. Her aunt had made sure of that. Boy, if Jonathan Kent ever needed a character witness, Molly knew just where to send him!

With a sigh, Molly threw on her clothes, braided her hair and headed for the kitchen.

"I've packed the basket for you, dear." Aunt Emily pulled off her apron and patted her hair. "If you don't mind, I think I'll get going now."

"Going?" Molly's ears perked up. "Where are you off to tonight?"

"Made some plans with Ralph and Alma, dear. Don't want to be late." With a breezy wave, Emily sailed through the kitchen and was out the front door before Molly had a chance to open her mouth.

"Try to stay out of trouble," she muttered, more to herself than to her aunt. She grabbed the picnic basket and hauled it to the living room. Her aunt must have packed enough food for an army; the basket weighed a ton.

Molly plopped down on the window seat, where she had a clear view of the street. What a beautiful night for a picnic, she thought, as she watched the setting sun spread a luminous glow across the early evening sky. Molly soaked up the view, letting the last rays of the sun warm her. She hadn't been on a picnic with a man in a long time. And she hadn't let one get close to her in a long time, either. Not until last night.

A frown marred her brow. Thinking about it, Molly realized that all the praise her aunt had given Jonathan didn't hide the fact that, in some ways, he was a lot like Paul. All the praise in the world couldn't erase the uneasy feeling she had about Jonathan. Or her suspicions.

Maybe if Jonathan had told her he had come home because he was worried about his grandmother, maybe then, she wouldn't have become so suspicious. But, from the vague and sketchy answers he had given her last night, she had a feeling he had come home to "take care" of his grandmother in much the same way Paul had wanted to take care of her aunt.

Anger began to bubble through her veins. Yet, it was hard for her to reconcile such a cold, indifferent attitude with the warm, caring man she had spent last evening with. But then again, Paul had had her fooled for a while, too.

She was smarter now, but obviously not smart enough to say no when Jonathan had asked her out again. What had she been thinking of? Her lips clamped into a thin line as self-annoyance burned through her. Why hadn't she simply shaken the man's hand and sent him on his way instead of walking willingly into his arms like a fly into a spider's web?

Well, she thought with sudden determination, she wouldn't make that mistake again. She would go on the picnic because, during a temporary lapse in common sense, she had agreed to. But, today, she was going to keep her wits about her and tell him that she wasn't going to see him again. She wasn't interested in getting involved in a relationship.

There was no denying that Jonathan Kent was a handsome, charming man, and no doubt some woman would be delighted to claim him for her own, but not this woman, Molly reminded herself firmly. She didn't want or need a man in her life. Molly took a deep breath. Now all she had to do was convince one gentle, redheaded giant.

"Yo, Mol-ly!"

The loud singsong yodel, reminiscent of her childhood, pierced the quiet evening air. Her startled gaze flew to the street, and she gasped. Jonathan was standing right below the window, an engaging smile on his face. The sight of him brought an unexpected flutter to her heart and her face grew warm.

Oh Lord, she thought, letting her eyes travel over him. He's gorgeous. Another sharp yodel pierced the air and she winced. Was the man crazy? The whole town had probably heard him yodeling for her like a ten-year-old.

She lifted her hand and waved, hoping it would quiet him down. But the sight of her only seemed to encourage him. Jonathan grinned broadly and waved back, singing out her name again.

Molly grabbed up the basket and nearly tripped over her own feet in her hurry to get to the front door. "Good Lord," she muttered. What on earth had she gotten herself into?

Chapter Five

Molly took the hall steps two at a time, juggling the basket and trying not to trip over her own feet. Jonathan Kent was totally exasperating, she thought, allowing a smile to lift her lips. Why did she have the feeling she was going out to play a game of kick the can instead of going out on a date?

Taking a deep breath, she threw open the front door and skidded full tilt into Jonathan, who was standing directly outside the door. Molly swallowed hard and let her gaze travel over him. He wore tattered sneakers, faded denims that looked wonderfully comfortable and fit his long, lean legs like a second skin, and a plaid shirt in shades of blue and green that picked up the color of his eyes and molded the well-muscled contours of his broad shoulders. Her gaze slid higher, and Molly's throat grew dry as her eyes finally settled on his smiling mouth.

"Hi, Molly." He looked genuinely pleased to see her and gave her a quick hug before taking the picnic basket out of her hand. "What a beautiful evening for a picnic. It's so warm that I thought we'd walk to the park. If I remember correctly, Dunsbar Park is just a few blocks from here." He draped an arm across her shoulder and she fell into step beside him, still a little stunned by his affectionate greeting.

"How do you know where the park is?" Her steps slowed, and she turned to face him, surprised by this sudden curve he had thrown her.

Jonathan laughed softly and gave her shoulder an affectionate squeeze. "I grew up in Hillchester."

She stopped abruptly and looked up at him, stunned. If Jonathan Kent had grown up in Hillchester surely she would have met him. And remembered him. Jonathan Kent was not the kind of man you forgot.

"You grew up here?" she repeated with raised brows. Jonathan urged her forward, steering her down the mossy green path that led into the park.

"Sure did. I'm not surprised you don't remember me. It's been a long time. I was about twelve the last time I saw you, and you were quite a bit younger, and if I remember correctly, you weren't interested in 'older men.'" He chuckled softly and Molly began to relax.

"You were cute as a button," he continued, taking her hand to walk along the narrowing path. She followed behind him, surprised at the way her hand fit perfectly into his. "Saucy little pigtails and a face full of adorable freckles."

"Go on," she urged, her curiosity aroused.

"It was at a picnic right here." Jonathan stopped at the top of the grassy knoll that overlooked the park. A honey-colored streak arched across the sky, touching the horizon as far as the eye could see. Puffs of clouds drifted aimlessly, their motion slow and lazy. It was totally quiet, except for the occasional squawking of a bird.

The knoll overlooked the large, grassy picnic area. Finally, after the long cold winter, the spring blossoms were bursting forth, turning the park from a dark, barren land into a garden of rich color. The pungent smell of freshly cut grass filled the air.

"This place hasn't changed that much," Jonathan said softly. Absently his fingers traced a delicate pattern atop her shoulder. "It's still beautiful. Almost as beautiful as you." He turned his head, and his gaze locked on hers, causing her breath to grow ragged. Molly made a conscious effort to breathe normally.

"Thank you," Molly muttered, pulling her eyes from him. It was not going to be easy to keep her well-intentioned resolutions if Jonathan was going to be so darn charming. Determined to change the mood and to get his attention off her, Molly gave him a playful poke in the ribs. "I'll race you down." Her eyes danced with delight.

"Is that a challenge, Miss Maguire?"

She nodded. It was no contest; she'd beat him handily. Molly had been running down this knoll since she was a kid. She knew every bump and groove in the ground. Besides, Jonathan was at a disadvantage. Even though he had longer legs, he was carrying the basket. But she wasn't about to tell him that.

"Molly, I think I should tell you. I simply can't resist a challenge." He smiled wickedly, and she wondered if there were a hidden meaning in his words. "You're on!" He took a giant step back, wrapping his fingers firmly around the leather strap of the picnic basket. "All right, now, when I give the signal, we go. Last one down has to clean up."

"Agreed." Molly nodded her head and stepped back until she was even with him. She tossed her braid behind her back and bounced on the soles of her feet in preparation.

"On your mark," he said slowly, poised in position and keeping his eyes on her. She tried not to smile. This was one challenge Jonathan Kent was going to lose. "Get set! Go!" He was off and running the moment the words were out.

He was two steps ahead of her before she even realized he had given the signal. "Foul!" she cried, scrambling down the grassy hill to catch up with him. She had almost reached him when Jonathan rolled forward and went head first the rest of the way down.

"Jonathan!" she cried in alarm as he landed in a tumbled heap on the grass at the bottom of the hill. "Jonathan?" She ran to him. "Are you all right?" Worry clouded her eyes, and she touched his shoulder.

He looked up and grinned. "Beat you!"

She drew back. "You did that on purpose? On purpose!" She gave his shoulder a hearty push.

"Of course." He grinned at the look on her face. "We agreed that the last one down cleans up. We didn't say you couldn't tumble down."

"You scared the daylights out of me. I thought you were hurt!" She was too relieved to be angry. When she had watched him tumble forward, her heart had caught in her throat; she'd been certain that he'd be injured.

Laughing softly, Jonathan lifted his arms and pulled her into his lap.

"Jonathan!" she cried in surprise. Her body reacted immediately to his nearness. She squirmed uncomfortably and glared into his smiling face.

"I never lose, Molly," he said softly, lifting a hand to brush back her hair. "Not when I want something."

Why did she get the feeling they weren't talking about a silly race down a hill? He loosened his hold for just a moment, and she scrambled to her feet.

She needed a moment to compose herself and to slow down her erratic breathing. His closeness, not to mention his comments, had made her uneasy. Was he trying to tell her something?

"What happened to the basket?" she asked, noticing for the first time that Jonathan didn't have it.

"Left it up there." He turned and pointed. Molly's gaze followed his finger, and there sat the picnic basket, safe and sound. He had this all planned! So much for trying to outsmart or best Jonathan Kent!

"You find a good spot, and I'll go retrieve the food." He held out a hand and she helped him up. Jonathan Kent was a force to be reckoned with, she realized as she watched him climb up the hill.

He was intimidating enough in her dreams and her thoughts, but she had forgotten how overwhelming the man actually was in person. And fun, her mind muttered. Molly scowled. She wouldn't think about that now.

"This spot is perfect, Molly." Startled, she whirled around. Jonathan was standing right behind her. His soft breath fanned the skin of her neck. Nervously, she pushed back her hair. He was just a bit too close for her comfort.

"Hungry?" She took a step forward and grabbed the basket from him. Without waiting for a response, she set the basket down and pulled out a large checkered blanket.

Jonathan dropped his long frame down beside her and watched as she snatched the containers of food out of the basket and laid them on the blanket.

"You didn't cook all this food, did you?" Jonathan grabbed a celery stalk and began to nibble.

"Of course, I did. I'll have you know I'm an excellent cook." Relieved that the conversation had finally settled on safer ground, Molly began to relax.

"Wonderful," he drawled softly. "You're an excellent cook. And I'm an excellent eater. We'll make a great team, Molly." His tone was mild, but she thought she detected a faint thread of commitment laced through his words.

Molly looked away and stared off into the distance. It was time for her to put her resolutions into actions. She had no wish to be part of any "team." She was strictly a solo act, and it was time to set Jonathan Kent straight on the matter.

"Jonathan," she began hesitantly, fingering a blade of grass, "I don't think . . . I don't think we should see each other anymore." He studied her intently, and Molly realized she had probably just failed tact and diplomacy.

Jonathan looked surprised. "Molly, don't you think that's a bit rash? If it will make you feel better, we can run the race over again, and this time I'll let you win. And I promise never to insult your cooking again. If it will help, I'll gladly eat every single morsel of food you've brought and enjoy every bit of it." He smiled into her uncertain face, and Molly couldn't help it: she smiled back.

She had to give the man an A for effort. Leave it to Jonathan to make light of the subject. He knew darn well her declaration had nothing to do with winning races or her culinary expertise. And she was not about to be put off so easily.

She lifted her eyes to his, determined to set him straight, but the warm smile on his face softened her resolve. "I just don't think it's a good idea, that's all."

"Are you afraid of me, Molly?" His fingers ran lightly up and down her arm, and she tried to ignore the pleasure she felt at his touch.

"No," she lied, pulling her eyes from his. *Terrified* was more like it, she thought. "I...I just don't want to get involved in a relationship right now."

"I'm glad to hear you're not afraid of me." His hand skated up her arm to cup her chin. She was forced to meet his eyes. The warmth and tenderness reflected in the depth of his gaze only frightened her more. "I won't hurt you, Molly," he whispered softly.

"Still—" Her voice froze. Where on earth was her resolve? More importantly, where on earth was her tongue? Somehow she had to find the courage to set him straight. Gently she pulled her chin free. "Jonathan, I just think it might be better not to get involved right now." She managed a casual tone, even though her pulse was doing a tango.

Jonathan sighed and rolled over on his back. He tucked his arms under his head and watched the clouds roll across the sky. "All right, Molly. If that's what you want."

His easy agreement was not quite what she expected and Molly eyed him suspiciously. She had lived with her aunt long enough to know when she was being led down the garden path.

"There's just one small problem, though." Jonathan turned his head to her. His lips were curved mischievously.

"Problem?" Molly frowned as a cloud of blankness settled over her. The feeling that Jonathan was up to something grew stronger. "What kind of problem?"

"Well, it seems to me that I promised your aunt I'd help her with the senior center. I'm a man of my word, Molly." His tone was serious, but she could see the faint laugh lines crinkling around his eyes.

"Jonathan, what has that got to do with me?" Her frown deepened.

"Well, if I'm to get anywhere in the little time that I'll be home, I'm going to need some help. I haven't lived here in a long time, Molly, and all the research that will be necessary could take days or even weeks unless I have some help. You know, Molly, someone who lives here and knows the area." He smiled innocently.

As casually as she could manage, she asked, "But certainly you must have secretaries to do that sort of thing?"

"Nope." His smile widened.

"Clerks?" she asked hopefully.

He shook his head happily. "Not a one."

"Anyone?" she croaked.

"Afraid not," he returned gleefully. "And, Molly, if I have to employ temporary help, who knows how much it would cost." He flashed her a triumphant smile, and her face fell.

"Did you have someone in mind?" she asked, wondering if she looked as dumb as she felt.

Jonathan was thoughtful. "Well, to tell you the truth, I was hoping for a volunteer. Unless of course you want me to tell your aunt that I couldn't help her because no one would help me."

Had he been taking lessons from Aunt Emily? she wondered dismally.

"Then, of course," he continued, struggling to keep a straight face, "there is the small matter of the two hundred dollars."

"Two hundred dollars?" she echoed faintly.

"Yes, I do believe that was the amount of Aunt Emily's bail. I'd be more than happy to verify the amount with Sheriff Pritchard if you like," he offered helpfully.

Molly groaned softly. The bail money! She hadn't even given it a thought. She'd been too wrapped up in her feelings about Jonathan to pay much attention to reality.

"I completely forgot about that," she returned sheepishly. Mentally she quickly calculated her bank balance and found it came out dismally short.

Molly silently cursed herself. Instead of daydreaming about Jonathan, she should have been trying to figure out a way to pay him back the money she owed him.

"Molly!" Jonathan's voice was scandalized. "Surely you don't want me to think you're the kind of woman who accepts a large sum of money from a man on a date and then tells him you don't want to see him again?"

"Jonathan Kent," she said with mock reproach, "you know very well that's not the way it was."

"Now, Molly, I know that." He sighed deeply and shook his head in an exaggerated gesture. "But someone else just might get the wrong idea. This is a small town, and people might talk." He clucked sympathetically. "Just think of what it could do to your reputation! On the other hand, if you were to volunteer to help me with the senior center, why, I think we could call that fair restitution of the debt.''

Looking at him, Molly realized he had successfully backed her into a corner and was taking full advantage of the situation. And enjoying himself immensely. Despite her misgivings about the man, she was flattered to think that he would go to such lengths to see her again. And she was certain that that was exactly what was behind this charade.

"Jonathan Kent—" she shook her finger at him "—that sounds suspiciously like blackmail!"

"I know."

"You should be ashamed of yourself," she scolded good-humoredly.

"I should be, but I'm not." He grinned. "Come on, Molly, what do you say? Is it a deal?" He looked so jubilant that suspicion clouded her eyes. She was out of her league, she realized suddenly. Jonathan Kent had an answer to everything, including questions she hadn't even asked yet! Molly wasn't at all certain that she could handle this man.

"Come here, girl," he commanded softly, grabbing her arm and tumbling her to the blanket. His body brushed against hers, sapping at her strength. She inhaled deeply, savoring the scent of him. He smelled so fresh, so masculine, that her pulse quivered in unspoken fear.

"J-Jonathan," she whispered, raising her hands to his chest. Through his shirt, she felt the warmth of his skin and the quick beat of his heart. Her senses went on red alert, warning her of the danger of having him so near.

Her tongue seemed paralyzed, a condition that was rapidly becoming a habit whenever Jonathan was around. She offered no protest as he lifted his hand to explore the contours of her face. An unwelcome surge of excitement warmed her. Jonathan's fingers, light as a feather, traced the outline of her mouth, and Molly held her breath in eager anticipation. A knot formed in the back of her throat as she watched his mouth lower toward hers. He glanced against her lips briefly, as if testing her resistance. Finding none, he buffeted her mouth with soft kisses.

Molly closed her eyes. She had to stop this. She had to stop *him*. Corralling her scattering thoughts, Molly tried again. "J-Jonathan," she began breathlessly. "I think ... I think it's important that we talk." Her eyes met his in desperate appeal.

"Talk? I thought that's what we were doing. All right, if you'd like to talk, we'll talk." Jonathan once again directed his attention to her mouth, which at the moment was hanging open. "Did you know I've always had a weakness for strawberry ice cream and beautiful brunettes? Not necessarily in that order, of course." Dipping his head, he dropped a gentle kiss on the hollow of her collarbone. Molly shifted, trying to evade his seeking lips. "And did you know that you have the most charming dimple right here on your chin?" His finger skipped over the spot, and her pulse reacted immediately, fluttering in passionate response.

"Did you also know that last night at dinner you ate your parsley garnish? I've never actually seen anyone do that, Molly. I was quite impressed." His voice dropped to a husky whisper. "I think I was hooked from that very moment."

He lowered his mouth slowly onto hers, and Molly's senses exploded in pleasure. His lips worked over hers with devastating leisureliness, and Molly responded—

much to her annoyance. She shifted her weight, trying to put some distance between them, but she succeeded only in molding herself more closely against him. Need soared through her, spiraling her into a world of exquisite delight. Her body tingled with awareness. When Jonathan kissed her, touched her or was even near her, she felt heady and breathless, almost as if she were in a falling elevator.

"Molly?" Jonathan slid his lips from hers and spoke against her cheek. "Don't look now, but I think we're the afternoon attraction." Molly blinked rapidly, trying to come back down to earth. Swallowing hard against a ridiculously racing pulse, she raised her eyes and gasped. The Simpson twins!

"Hello, Miss Maguire." They giggled in unison. Wide-eyed, the two stood at the edge of the blanket. Judging from the looks on their faces, they were enjoying the show.

With a barely muffled groan, Molly pushed Jonathan away and sat up, struggling to straighten her clothes in the process. She tried to pretend she was in total control, but her hands were shaking, to say nothing of her heart.

"Hello, children," she said, fussily smoothing back her hair and cursing the surge of heat that coursed into her cheeks.

Identical from their mops of golden curls to the gap each had between their two front teeth, the six-year-old twins poked each other and giggled. "Hi," they repeated, taking a step closer to inspect Jonathan.

"Hi, kids," he caroled brightly. "We're having a picnic. Want to join us?" Molly turned to glare at him, but he paid no heed. "We've got fried chicken and potato salad, and I think we've even got some homemade

apple pie." Jonathan started digging through the containers of food, totally oblivious of Molly's discomfort.

"No thank you, sir," Mark returned, shaking his
blond head. "We have to get going. We're late for dinner." He grabbed his sister's arm and tried to drag her
away, but Martha seemed more interested in Jonathan
than in going home for dinner.

"Martha," Mark growled, grabbing his sister's arm
and giving it a good tug. "Come on! We're late. Good
night Miss Maguire," he said politely. Martha just
grinned. Her eyes were pinned to Jonathan. Molly knew
how she felt. It was hard to pay attention to anything
else with Jonathan around. Obviously even kindergar-
teners weren't immune to the man's charms.

With a final tug, Mark managed to get his sister
moving. But Martha kept looking back at them, an im-
pish smile on her six-year-old face.

"Cute kids," Jonathan commented, peeking at the
food.

Molly turned to stare at him. Cute kids? Cute kids!
That was all he had to say? How could the man sit there
so calmly? She was still reeling from the impact of his
kiss.

Another thought crowded her mind and she swallowed a moan. The twins! No doubt they had raced
home to report that they had caught their teacher wres-
tling around on a blanket with a strange man in the
park. Molly lifted her shoulders and sighed. Mrs.
Simpson, the twins' mother, wasn't known as Cyanide
Simpson because of her charitable disposition or her
sweet tongue. If the whole town didn't already know
that she and Jonathan had been caught necking in the

park, they would by morning if Mrs. Simpson had her way.

"Something wrong, Molly? You've got that frown again." Jonathan looked at her curiously, his eyes darkened in concentration.

Molly squared her shoulders and struggled to clear her muddled thoughts. Now that she had Jonathan's full attention, she had to set him straight, once and for all. The entire situation was getting out of hand.

Turning to him, she did her best to ignore his bright smile. It was time for her to be strong. "Jonathan, we've got to get a few things straight." Molly forced herself to meet his glittering gaze and nearly lost her courage. She rushed on. "I'm sorry about the bail money. I really did forget about it. I'll be more than happy to help you with the senior center. After all, you are doing it for my aunt." Jonathan opened his mouth to speak, but Molly lifted her hand. She had to get the words out now before she lost what little courage she had left. "Please, let me finish. I think you should know that I'll agree to this on the condition that we remain strictly friends." She twisted the edge of the blanket, mentally forming the words she would need to counter the protest she was certain would be forthcoming.

Jonathan shrugged and smiled. "Sounds good to me."

Molly's mouth fell open and she nearly choked. Jonathan never failed to surprise her. His ready agreement was the last thing she'd expected. Was he up to something else? she wondered, watching him through narrowed eyes.

He rocked back and grinned at her. "I've got just one more question, Molly."

One perfectly arched brow rose. Here it comes, she thought. "What's that?"

"Can we eat now? I'm starving."

Chapter Six

More chicken?" Molly asked, wiping her hands on a napkin.

Jonathan groaned and rubbed his stomach. "I couldn't eat another bite, Molly. You're a great cook." A satisfied smile lifted his lips.

Molly smiled back and she basked in the warmth of his compliment. Jonathan had a terrific appetite, though she wondered where on earth he put all that food. There wasn't an ounce of fat on the man anywhere. She knew, for she had been carefully checking him out all evening.

Jonathan settled himself comfortably on the blanket. "I can't wait to discover your other hidden talents," he drawled softly as he helped himself to another glass of lemonade.

Molly smiled. "I don't have any hidden talents," she insisted, taking the refill of lemonade he offered. His fingers brushed hers, and instinctively she pulled back her hand, but not before a warm tingle skated up her arm. "Unless you count being able to understand Aunt Emily."

Jonathan laughed. "Come on, Molly, don't be modest," he coaxed. "You're a beautiful woman, great company and a terrific cook. There must be more to Molly Margaret Maguire than that." His gaze slid slowly over her, and she felt herself stiffen at the surge of heat that burst through her senses. When he looked at her like that, she felt all . . . addled.

"How do you know my middle name?" she asked suspiciously. She didn't remember telling him all that much about herself, and certainly hadn't told him her middle name. She rarely told *anyone* her middle name.

"Ahhh," he drawled, managing a pretty good leer. "I know a great deal about the woman named Molly Margaret Maguire. But not nearly as much as I'd like," he finished seriously.

Molly studied the expression on his face, and her heart pumped just a bit faster. "Jonathan." She sighed in exasperation. The man was impossible. "I thought we agreed, just friends, remember?"

He held up his hand to silence her. "We did agree, but as your friend, aren't I entitled to know a little more about you?" He was giving her one of those innocent smiles again, and Molly wondered if she was being just a bit touchy.

"What would you like to know?" she asked, groping for a light, friendly tone.

Folding his arms behind his head, he turned to study her intently. Molly wished his all-encompassing attention wasn't focused so much on her. "Well, for starters, do you like children?"

"Children?" She laughed. He was off in another direction again. That wasn't exactly the kind of question she'd expected and a relieved sigh escaped her. At least they seemed to finally be on neutral ground. "Yes, I adore children. I guess that's why I became a teacher. I've got twenty more just like the Simpson twins in my kindergarten class. Not all twins, of course."

"Sounds like you enjoy your work."

Molly smiled. "I love it."

His eyes roamed over her again, settling on her mouth, and Molly had the distinct feeling she had just experienced the softest whisper of a kiss.

"You love your work? And you love children?" She nodded. Jonathan seemed to be taking her comments under advisement. "Then why haven't you ever married?"

Her smile faded and a flutter of tension stiffened her spine. Jonathan's choice of subject matter seemed to come from left field. He jumped from subject to subject without any rhyme or reason. Was it to keep her off balance? she wondered. What her work and her students had to do with marriage, she'd never know. And she wasn't about to ask. Every time she thought they were on safe ground once again, Jonathan would drop the floor out from under her by introducing a new and usually touchy subject.

Standing abruptly, she brushed off her jeans. "Let's go for a walk, shall we?"

Jonathan uncoiled himself and rose to his feet. "Anything you say." He swung into step beside her and firmly took her hand in his.

With a determined effort, Molly ignored the forced closeness and kept her voice steady and impersonal. "The park is really beautiful this time of year," she commented as they made their way down a narrow shrub-lined path. "This is my favorite time of year," she remarked quietly. "The flowers are just beginning to blossom, and the grass is finally green again after the long cold winter."

"Got anything nice to say about the dirt?" Jonathan bent and picked up a handful, letting it drift slowly through his fingers.

Molly blinked in confusion. Now what the devil was the man talking about? "What?"

"Since you're giving me a detailed description of the landscape, I thought you might want to add something nice about the dirt." Mischief danced in his eyes as he looked down at her, and Molly realized she hadn't fooled him for a minute.

"Well, it's nice and black," she returned seriously.

"Yes, it is. Rather dry, though." Jonathan turned his head to survey the park, pretending to be desperately impressed with the surroundings. "Do you come here often?" he inquired politely.

Molly shook her head. "Not as often as I'd like. I bring my children here every year for our school picnic. Right beyond that clump of trees is a small playground with swings. The children love it."

"Swings?" Jonathan's brows rose. "Did you say swings?" At her nod, he tightened his grip on her hand. "What are we waiting for? Let's go." He broke into a run, pulling her along.

"Stop! Jonathan!" she cried breathlessly, pausing to catch her breath. "I can't run that fast." With an ease that astounded her, Jonathan scooped her up in his arms and continued to run, oblivious to her wild shrieks.

Pressed tightly against his hard body, she couldn't find any place to put her arms except around his muscular neck. Her fingers itched to slide through the luxuriant strands of his hair, but she restrained herself. The scent of him was dizzying, and she closed her eyes, willing the feelings of pleasure that rolled through her to retreat.

With less effort than she could have believed, Jonathan continued to sprint, oblivious of the weight she added.

"Jonathan, stop. What will people think?" Her eyes darted about. She wouldn't have been at all surprised to find Mrs. Simpson hiding in the bushes with a camera.

"People will think that we're..." His voice trailed off. "People will think that we're friends," he announced as he set her down gently on the swing. His eyes found hers, and Molly's senses reeled.

"Now, I'll push first," he informed her. "Then it's your turn. I want you to know, Molly Margaret Maguire, that I am a liberated man. Equal rights and equal pushes."

Laughing, Molly clung tightly to the ropes of the swing as she soared higher and higher until she was nearly breathless. "Jonathan," she cried over her shoulder, "not so high. I'm going to fall." The wind rushed against her face, and her hair streamed out behind her.

Jonathan abruptly reached out and grabbed the seat of the swing, bringing her slowly and steadily to a halt. Sliding his hands to her slender waist, he lifted her carefully off the swing and set her down in front of him.

"Molly," he said softly, giving her shoulders a gentle squeeze, "you don't ever have to worry about falling when I'm around. Not off swings, or anything else."

His hands, warm and gentle, caressed her shoulders, and she tried not to look up at him. His touch was affecting her again.

Looking into those eyes was dangerous, she realized. It did something to her inner system—something that she wasn't certain she could handle at the moment.

"Did you hear me?" Jonathan cupped her chin, stroking her gently.

Trembling, she looked up into his gentle eyes. Something was stirring inside of her, something she tried to ignore. "Jonathan, please." Her voice had taken on a helpless, pleading tone.

"Molly, listen to me."

She had no choice in the matter. She was his captive audience. She couldn't walk away if she wanted to. Her legs didn't seem to be getting the message her mind was sending.

"Something or someone has hurt you deeply, but don't be afraid of me. *I* won't hurt you, not ever." His voice was a hushed whisper, and she found herself shivering in spite of the warmth of the evening.

Jonathan's gaze caressed her upturned face. A pulsating sensation dropped her stomach and she gulped as his parted lips descended toward hers.

"J-Jonatha—" His mouth cut off her words as his lips claimed hers in a sweet, gentle kiss. Her hands slowly moved up Jonathan's back, coming to rest on the broad width of his shoulders. Their breaths mingled as she opened her lips greedily.

Jonathan lifted his mouth and gathered her close in his arms. "Don't be afraid of me," he whispered against her hair. "I promise I won't hurt you."

Dazed, Molly leaned against him, no longer able to fight the feelings that tore through her with agonizing speed. Jonathan's fingers lazily trailed up and down her back. His lips traveled a path of their own, from the pulse at her temple, down to the soft area of her cheek, finally coming to rest once again on her waiting lips. With a sigh, Molly closed her eyes and gave in to the heady feeling of the moment, letting her emotions overrule her intellect.

She hungrily kissed him back. Burning shivers of joy caused her spirit to soar.

"Molly?" Jonathan grumbled softly, lifting his head. "Either a bird has deposited something terribly distasteful on my head, or it's raining."

"What?" Her lids lifted slowly. Raising her head, she saw that the sky, which had been Wedgwood blue, had turned dark and ominous. "It's raining," she groaned, pulling her arms down to where they belonged. "We'd better get back."

Jonathan scowled at the darkened sky as a clap of thunder broke loose. "Let's make a run for it." Racing down the path, Jonathan caught her hand in his as she struggled to keep up with him.

The rainstorm was nothing compared to the private storm brewing inside Molly. Her senses were still swirling. Her heart pumped for all it was worth, and her lips longed for the sweet taste of Jonathan.

He clutched her hand tightly as they bobbed and weaved along the rain-soaked path, sidestepping mud puddles. Laughing, they quickly threw the soggy picnic gear into the basket before racing on.

"Molly?" Jonathan said, panting and pushing his wet hair off his face. "You know what I'd really love right now?"

"An umbrella?" she asked. Her foot landed in a deep puddle of muddy water and she groaned.

Jonathan shook his head and laughed. "No, ice cream."

"Ice cream?" she echoed in disbelief. Her sandals were soaked, and they squeaked with each clumsy step. A trickle of mud oozed between her toes as she tried to keep up with Jonathan's long strides. Her hair was plastered against her head, and cool droplets of water slid down her white cotton shirt, which was now thoroughly drenched and clung provocatively to every curve. They were about to drown, and he wanted ice cream!

"Jonathan," she protested, slowing down a bit to catch her breath, "I can't go anywhere looking like this."

Jonathan stopped and let his eyes roam over her. "Looking like what?" He looked genuinely perplexed and Molly smiled.

"Like this." She grinned and pulled the cotton shirt from her skin. It was nearly transparent and she flushed as his eyes slid over her curves again. "I'm soaked," she whispered hoarsely.

"You'll dry off."

"I—I'm cold." She shivered, trying to ward off the mesmerizing pull of his eyes. He was overwhelming her again.

"I'll keep you warm," he offered, dropping an arm around her shoulder and tucking her into the circle of his arms. That was what she'd been afraid of. Her temperature seemed to soar to a fevered pitch whenever Jonathan was around, and she felt helpless to control it. Worse, she was no longer sure she wanted to.

Jonathan tightened his arms around her, then kissed the tip of her cold nose. "Molly, unless you say yes, we're both going to drown."

"All right." She laughed. "Yes, yes. Ice cream is fine. Strawberry if you insist. But lets get out of this rain." She grabbed his hand and started running, slipping and sliding along the path.

The downpour let up just as they reached the ice-cream parlor.

"Great timing," Jonathan teased, pulling open the door and shaking himself off. He gave her back end a playful pat as she scooted past him.

"Jonathan!" she muttered as she stepped around him.

"Grandmother! Miss Emily! Ralph!" Jonathan's cheerful voice boomed through the parlor. Molly tried to look inconspicious as every head seemed to turn in their direction. "How nice to see you."

Her eyes widened at the trio who were sitting in a booth near the back of the restaurant. Jonathan headed straight for them, pulling up two chairs. "Come on, Molly, sit down." He patted the chair next to him and tucked the soggy basket under his seat. "We had a picnic supper," he informed the trio. "We decided to stop for some ice cream." Three pairs of curious eyes stared at Molly and Jonathan.

"At least you had the good sense to come in out of the rain," Aunt Emily commented, giving Molly a benevolent smile.

"Grandmother, what are you eating?" Jonathan reached across the table and dipped his finger into the frothy concoction his grandmother had in front of her. "Mmm," he murmured, rolling his eyes, "it's wonderful. Think I'll have the same. In strawberry. How about you Molly?" He turned to her and winked.

Pushing a tumble of wet hair off her face, Molly laughed. "That's fine, Jonathan. I'll have whatever you're having."

Ralph Pritchard, who had been silently staring at the pair, nudged Emily. "It's about time that girl found herself another beau," he whispered loudly enough for everyone at the table and probably half the parlor to hear. A heated flush climbed Molly's cheeks, and she glared at Ralph, but he ignored her and continued smiling broadly at her aunt.

Jonathan grinned at Ralph's comments and draped an arm around the back of Molly's chair. "Isn't that the truth, Ralph?" he agreed sympathetically. "I was just telling Molly she'd better hurry up and find a man before she's too old. Why, I hear she's almost twenty-six." Jonathan's voice had dropped to a scandalous whisper, and Molly searched for his shin under the table.

"Jonathan," she whispered. "Don't encourage him."

"Time's running out, Molly," Jonathan teased with a wicked grin.

Why did she ever agree to come for ice cream? she wondered. And why on earth had she ever agreed to go out with this madman?

"Plenty of time left." Emily sniffed. "Why, her mother didn't marry until she was nearly twenty-eight."

Marry? Marry! Rolling her eyes skyward, Molly sunk lower in her chair. Two dates with the man, and they had her married. It was time to change the subject, before they began writing out wedding invitations and naming the children.

"Aunt Emily?" Molly directed her attention to her aunt and tried to force her voice to a normal tone. "I've agreed to help Jonathan look into the problems at the senior center."

Her aunt smiled sweetly, but Molly didn't miss the silent glances the trio exchanged. She eyed them carefully. Why did she have the feeling that her announcement was not news to them?

"You're such a good girl, Molly. I'm sure Jonathan will be able to use your help." It was Alma's only contribution to the conversation so far, yet it was almost the same line, word for word, that Jonathan had used. Either the same thought patterns ran through their genes, or his grandmother had been coaching him. When she saw Jonathan duck his head to hide a smile, Molly suspected the latter.

"First thing Monday, we're going to start, aren't we, Molly?" Jonathan gave her shoulder an affectionate squeeze, and Molly winced as all eyes turned to them. She felt uncomfortable under the trio's scrutiny.

"You may be on vacation, Jonathan, but I've got classes to teach Monday," Molly returned stiffly. Did he have to sit so close? And keep his arm around her?

"Wanna play hooky?" he asked, his mouth curling into a mischievous grin.

"No, I don't," she returned, giving him a look that she usually reserved for misbehaving students. Molly scooted forward a bit in her chair, but Jonathan's hand reached out and captured her shoulder, pulling her back so that she was nearly resting against him. The man was impossible, she decided, but he *was* warm, and her chilled body reacted to the heat of his.

Determined to ignore the magnetism that was drawing her closer to Jonathan, Molly turned her attention to Ralph. "Did Aunt Emily tell you Clarence arrested her last night?"

"Heard all about it, missy. That boy of mine does get carried away at times. He meant no harm, but I'll have a talk with him just the same. We owe your new beau a debt of gratitude for bailing Miss Emily out—not that Clarence wouldn't have let her go sooner or later." Ralph's voice rose an octave, and Molly winced at the word he'd used. Her new beau? Everyone was acting as if she and Jonathan were joined at the hip! And what was with Ralph? For a man who still kept his sons in line despite the fact that they were grown and on their own, he was acting very peculiar.

"Well, children, we've got to be going now. We've got a few things to do." Aunt Emily abruptly pushed her glass away and pulled on her raincoat.

Things to do? Molly looked at the three of them. Something was up; she could feel it in her bones. Lord, she only hoped it didn't land them all in jail this time!

"Where are you going?" Molly asked, looking at the three of them. The trio exchanged another silent glance, and Molly stifled a groan. "You're not planning on doing any more picketing, are you?"

"Picketing?" Emily smiled and Molly cringed. That smile again! "Whatever gave you that idea?" Emily's brows furrowed in surprise, and she looked at Molly as if she had finally gone round the bend.

"Come on Ralph, Alma, let's go," Emily urged them on, and Jonathan stood to allow them an easier exit. Bending over to kiss his grandmother's cheek, he whispered something in her ear that Molly couldn't make out, but it brought a wide smile to Alma's face. Saying their goodbyes, the trio weaved their way out of the restaurant.

Molly slid into the booth, her brows gathered in thought. "They are definitely up to something, and I don't like it one bit." Absently she tapped her finger against her lip, her thoughts racing.

"Relax, Molly, they're all grown-ups. They're perfectly capable of taking care of themselves." Jonathan reached across the table and patted her hand.

Molly's mind snapped to attention as a streak of annoyance raced through her. Was this the same man who had just told her the night before that he had come home because he was worried about his grandmother living alone? Now he was telling her she was perfectly capable of taking care of herself. What kind of game was he playing with her? She narrowed her gaze and looked at him carefully.

"Funny you should say that. Aren't you the one who came home to *take care* of your grandmother? I guess she can take care of herself when it suits your purpose." Her voice rose as her temper flared.

Jonathan leaned back in the booth and stared at her, a look of surprise on his face. "Whoa, Molly." He raised his hand, his eyes questioning. "Where did that come from?"

His look of innocence only sparked her temper. "Jonathan, I *know* why you've come home," she accused, trying to keep the anger out of her voice.

"Of course, you do. I told you why last night." He picked up the ice-cream menu and began to look it over.

She glared at him across the table. Was he deliberately trying to aggravate her? "No, Jonathan. I mean, I know the real reason why you've come home."

"Hmm," he commented, lifting his head a fraction. "Molly, what's wrong? That frown's about to become permanent." He looked at her carefully. "What do you mean, 'the real reason'?" It was his turn to frown.

"Jonathan, I may live in a small town, but I'm no yokel," she snapped. "I know exactly what you're up to."

"What I'm up to?" Jonathan shook his head. "Maybe I'm the yokel, Molly, but I don't have the faintest idea what you're talking about."

Taking a deep breath, she squared her shoulders. There was no use pretending. He might as well know she was on to him. "I know you've come home to put your grandmother away somewhere." Just saying the words made fury bubble through her veins.

Jonathan burst out laughing. "What!"

His laughter fueled her anger, and she stiffened. "I hardly think this is a laughing matter, Jonathan," she returned curtly.

One brow rose and he shook his head. "Where on earth did you ever get an idea like that?"

"Where did I get the idea?" she roared in disbelief. "From your own mouth, last night!"

Jonathan cocked his head, his eyes intent on hers. "Either I have amnesia, Molly, or your ears aren't in working order. I don't remember ever telling you I came home 'to put my grandmother away somewhere.'"

Her eyes narrowed and she glared at him. "Jonathan Kent! Last night you told me—"

He raised his hand to silence her. "Last night, I told you a lot of things, and I meant each and every one of them. But I did *not* tell you that I came home to put my grandmother away somewhere."

Maybe he hadn't said it in so many words, but she knew what she'd heard. And what he'd meant. Why was he trying to deny it? "Then you *are* going to move her to Portland?"

Jonathan shook his head. "No, I told you last night, Molly, I'm not going to move my grandmother to Portland. She doesn't want to move to Portland. I love my grandmother, Molly," he added softly. "I only want what's best for her."

What was best for her. His words struck a raw nerve. It was the same line Paul had used on her about Aunt Emily. Molly struggled to hold on to her dwindling composure. Naturally he would assume that only he knew what was best for his grandmother!

"Jonathan, let me see if I've got this straight. You love your grandmother—"

"Yes, I love my grandmother," he repeated.

"You're concerned about her living alone." She waited for his nod before she continued. "But you're not going to move her to Portland?"

Jonathan smiled. "You've got it."

"Then what the devil is going to happen to her?" she bellowed, not caring that she was showing her temper.

"Nothing." He shook his head and laughed, causing another surge of anger to rock her. "Absolutely nothing."

Her eyes widened. Did he really expect her to believe this nonsense? Why was he deliberately being evasive? she wondered. What was he trying to hide? "I'm supposed to believe—"

"Molly," he growled, "do you honestly think I'm going to come charging into my grandmother's life and start making her decisions for her?" He sounded incredulous, and Molly's eyes narrowed suspiciously.

"I don't know what to think."

He shook his head wearily. "If I gave you the impression I came home to rearrange my grandmother's life to suit me, I'm sorry." His shoulders lifted, and he offered her a wan smile, but Molly still wasn't convinced. Something still didn't ring true.

"Last night you said you were working on a few things. What things?" If the man's intentions toward his grandmother were truly honorable why didn't he just tell her what he was up to and be done with it? What the devil was the big secret?

Jonathan looked at her for a long moment. "You don't believe me, do you? You don't believe one word I've said!" The look he gave her made Molly flush, and she realized how transparent her feelings were.

"A relationship can't possibly go anywhere without trust, Molly," he said softly, reaching out to cover her hand with his.

She yanked her hand free. His touch was disturbing. It wasn't easy to think clearly when Jonathan touched her, and she needed to think clearly.

Shaking her head, Molly tried to clear her thoughts. A moment ago they were talking about his grandmother. Now Jonathan was suddenly talking about a relationship. Why did he deliberately change the subject whenever his grandmother came up? He did that last night, she remembered. Why?

"I don't want a relationship, Jonathan," she said carefully. "I thought you understood that. You agreed we could just remain friends."

"Even friends have to trust each other."

Trust. The word almost choked her as a haze of fury blurred her vision. That was what it was all about. Now she understood. He wanted her to trust him, simply because he said so. She had once trusted a man, solely on his word. She wasn't about to make that mistake again. Jonathan had not given her one solid reason to trust him. All he had done was give her more reasons to be suspicious and doubtful of him.

"Trust!" Molly cried. "You expect me to trust you when you won't even give me a straight answer! You claim to love your grandmother, and you're worried about her living alone, but you're not going to move her to Portland. You're working on 'something,' but you won't tell me what! Based on all of that, you expect me to trust you?" Her tone was incredulous.

"You really think I've come home to put my grandmother away, don't you?" he asked, and Molly shuddered. That was exactly what she thought.

"My God, what kind of man do you think I am?" His voice rose in disbelief and Molly looked away. "I don't believe this!" he growled, tossing his napkin to the table in disgust. "Molly, if you really think I'm such a monster, why don't you just notify Sheriff Pritchard? Tell him that big, bad Jonathan Kent is in town. Maybe you'd better warn all the little old ladies in town while you're at it."

"Come on." Jonathan slid from the booth and stood up. "I'll take you home. You might not be safe with the likes of me." His mouth tugged downward in an angry frown.

With great dignity, Molly squared her shoulders. "No, thank you," she said with forced politeness. "I know the way." She lifted her chin to a defiant angle, and with her eyes straight ahead, she swept past Jonathan and marched from the restaurant.

Chapter Seven

"Good morning, dear. Did you sleep well?" Emily poured herself a cup of coffee and joined Molly at the kitchen table.

Molly's fingers tensed on her cup. She hadn't slept well in two days, not since she'd stormed out on Jonathan at the ice-cream parlor.

She was rumpled and tired, even though she had just spent eight hours in bed. Eight sleepless, restless hours. She'd been exhausted but hadn't been able to sleep. Every time she'd closed her eyes, Jonathan had been there.

Suppressing a yawn, Molly smiled. "Yes," she lied, feeling a twinge of guilt. She couldn't ever remember lying to her aunt, and she certainly didn't like doing so now, but she didn't want to worry her. "Very well. How about you?"

Emily nodded and kept her eyes fixed on Molly. Self-consciously Molly lowered her gaze to scowl into her cup. Jonathan Kent didn't even have the decency to leave her alone in her misery. And, she realized with a touch of resentment, that's exactly what she was: miserable.

Over and over again she had mentally replayed their harsh words. Such a beautiful day had turned into a nightmare.

"Haven't seen Jonathan around, dear. Did you two have a lovers' spat?"

Molly nearly choked on her aunt's choice of words. "Aunt Emily," she said softly. "Jonathan and I are hardly lovers."

"Then you did have a spat?" Emily's eyes pinned her, and Molly shifted uncomfortably. She couldn't very well tell her aunt that what she and Jonathan had had was more a battle than a spat. If she admitted such a thing, Aunt Emily would want to know just what they had to argue about, and Molly certainly couldn't tell her. How could she admit that she suspected that 'for her own good' Jonathan was about to shuffle his grandmother off someplace away from her home and her family, not to mention her friends?

A tremor of anxiety skated up her spine. She wasn't about to tell her aunt about her suspicions. Why alarm her?

Besides, Molly reasoned, taking a long sip of her coffee, there was always the outside chance that she had been wrong about Jonathan and his intentions. She realized it was a slim chance, but a chance nonetheless. And until she was absolutely certain, she couldn't worry her aunt needlessly. She'd tell her when the time came and not a moment sooner.

"Well?" Emily persisted. "Did you have a spat?"

Molly set her cup down and carefully chose her words. "I'm sure Jonathan has just been busy."

"Busy, huh?" Emily's brows rose, and a hiss of breath whistled from her pursed lips, but thankfully she said nothing more.

Clinging to her composure, Molly drained her cup and set it in the sink. "I've got to get dressed for school. I don't want to be late." She pecked her aunt's cheek and hurried from the room, ignoring the look in her aunt's eyes.

All that day Molly tried to immerse herself in her students. She patiently colored and cut and she answered in a great deal more detail than necessary every question asked. She wanted to keep busy to keep her mind occupied and off Jonathan Kent.

It didn't work. Just the sight of the Simpson twins brought back a flood of memories of Jonathan and the picnic supper they had shared. Even her suspicions didn't stop the memories. If she closed her eyes, she could see his irresistible grin, smell the scent of him, hear his rich laughter.

Not that she actually missed him, she told herself. That was totally ridiculous. How could she miss a man she barely knew? Easy, her mind muttered. Maybe the length of time she had known Jonathan hadn't been too long, but somehow, instinctively, she knew him. Perhaps it was better this way, she rationalized. She didn't want a man in her life. Not even one with laughing eyes.

The day ended all too soon, leaving Molly alone with time on her hands. She didn't quite feel up to going home yet. She wasn't certain she could face her aunt or any more questions about Jonathan. Moving through her empty classroom, Molly busied herself wiping finger paints off the desks. Gaily colored pictures the children had painted were spread across her table to dry. Grabbing a rag, Molly scrubbed a blob of yellow paint off one of the desks, certain there was more paint on the desk than on the pictures.

A faint knock at the door caught her attention, and she sighed inwardly. She really wasn't up to any conferences today, but the parents of her students knew she was always available after school, no matter what the problem. Wiping a spatter of paint off her hands, Molly turned toward the door and faked her best teacher's smile.

"Come in," she called gaily.

The door opened slowly and a small white flag waved breezily around the door, bringing a curious smile to her lips. "Is it safe? Can I come in?" Jonathan's voice caressed her starved senses, bringing an unexpected lift to her heart. Quickly she brushed back her hair and smoothed down her painting smock.

"Of course, you can come in, Jonathan." Molly cursed the sudden tremor in her voice. Not wanting to appear anxious, Molly rounded her desk, grabbed a few pictures and pretended to examine them.

"Hi, Molly." Jonathan peeked his head around the door and waved the flag in her general direction. Her eyes drank him in. "A peace offering." He stepped around the door and flashed a dazzling smile. "I wanted to be sure I wasn't going to get clobbered before I came in." He pulled his other hand from behind his back and handed her a bouquet of fresh spring flowers.

"Jonathan, they're lovely," she whispered, touched by his thoughtfulness. Molly bent and took a deep whiff of the fragrant blooms. She deliberately kept her eyes from his. She didn't want him to see the sudden joy she felt. Didn't want him to know how glad she was to see him.

"Molly, I'm sorry about the other night." He grinned boyishly. "The more I thought about it, the more I realized how you could have misinterpreted what I said about my grandmother. I apologize." His smile was warm and sincere.

Molly looked at him carefully, and a flicker of doubt planted itself firmly in her mind. Had she misinterpreted what Jonathan had said? Was it possible she was wrong about him? She couldn't be sure anymore.

"Are you ready, Molly?" His eyes twinkled at her sudden look of amazement. He was doing it to her again.

"Ready? For what?"

"For what? Molly Maguire, don't tell me you've forgotten our date."

"Date?" she echoed faintly. Jonathan's disjointed sentences and abrupt changes of subject matter were playing havoc with her mind. She hadn't made a date with him. Or had she? He could have told her she had volunteered to ride shotgun on a spaceship, and she probably would have believed him. Since meeting him, she had agreed to do a lot of things she wouldn't have believed she'd do. Like prancing around in the rain, necking in the park and Lord knows what else.

"The senior center, remember? We've got to get to work. Time's running out. I'm due back in Portland in less than ten days." His words caused her heart to hammer. Portland. She'd completely forgotten about the blasted place. Just the sound of the word made her ill. The thought of Jonathan leaving brought a strong bout of sadness, and she didn't know why.

Jonathan leaned against the desk and looked at her affectionately. "I thought we'd grab a bite to eat first."

Molly shook her head. Helping him as she'd promised was one thing, but she wasn't about to let this turn into a real date. She had to keep her wits about her, not an easy task with him around. Jonathan would be leaving soon and she was already more attached to the man than she cared to admit. If she allowed her feelings to continue unchecked, his departure in ten days— Molly shook the thought from her mind. She didn't even want to think about it. It shouldn't bother her that he was leaving in less than two hundred and forty hours. But it did.

"Jonathan, I don't think I can." His eyes widened in surprise, and she rushed on. "Eat, that is." Who could concentrate on food with him around, anyway?

His lips twitched innocently. "Sure you can. It's easy. First you open your mouth. Then you put the food in and chew. It's really very simple. I've been doing it quite a while now. I'll be happy to show you how."

She opened her mouth to protest again, then promptly snapped it shut. The look on his face was so appealing that her resistance melted. She did have to eat, didn't she? "All right," she finally conceded.

He flashed her a dazzling smile. "That's my girl."

His words made her stiffen. "Jonathan," she said carefully, "I'm not a girl, and I'm not yours." The term always grated on her nerves. Jonathan had no way of knowing that Paul had always called her "his girl." "I'm a woman. My own woman."

"Ooops! Sorry, slip of the tongue." He waved the flag in the air again. "Tell you what, just to prove I believe that you are your own woman, I'll let you pay for your own dinner. How's that?"

Molly laughed softly. He was totally impossible, not to mention irresistible. "You've got a deal. Let me just finish up here." Turning her attention to her table, Molly quickly gathered the paintings and clipped them on the bulletin board to dry. She enjoyed displaying her students' work. It allowed her to see just how far they had progressed since the beginning of the year.

"Nice pictures," Jonathan commented, cocking his head to get a better look. "I particularly like the one that's green and black all over. Kind of looks like an avocado that's been stomped on."

Molly laughed and turned back to Jonathan, and her eyes widened in delight. "What on earth are you doing?"

He had twisted his long frame to fit into one of the children's chairs. Seeing him coiled in the tiny seat brought a smile to her face. "We may not be able to get you out of that," she warned, shaking her head.

"Nonsense." He squirmed uncomfortably. "I'm just a kindergartener at heart. Although at the moment, I think my heart is about the only thing that *is* kindergarten size. Maybe you'd better help me up."

Molly reached out and hauled Jonathan from the seat, acutely aware of the warmth that bolted through her at his touch. He groaned softly and rubbed his backside. "Now I know how poor Sheriff Pritchard felt."

Laughing, Molly quickly removed her smock and smoothed down her red cotton dress, wondering why she hadn't worn something a bit more attractive today.

"Come on, Molly, let's go eat." Jonathan grabbed her hand and led her out of the building. The touch of his hand warmed her senses. She couldn't deny it any longer: she enjoyed being with Jonathan. When he was

near, the sun seemed to shine just a bit brighter. Molly
realized she no longer cared if the whole town saw them
together. She was just glad he was there.

"Penny for your thoughts." Something in his voice
caused her to raise her eyes to his.

"Oh, it's nothing," she lied, realizing her thoughts,
not to mention her mind, had suddenly become soft
when it came to him. "I was just trying to decide where
to eat. What do you feel like?" Smiling, she gazed up
at him. Oh how she'd missed him!

"Actually, I feel quite wonderful. Here, touch."
Jonathan stopped abruptly and before she could protest, captured her hand and slowly lifted it to his lips.

"Jonathan! That's not what I meant and you know
it." She snatched her hand back and tried to look
properly affronted. Did the man have to take everything she said literally?

"I missed you, Molly," he whispered. "I haven't
been able to stop thinking about you." His eyes
searched her face. The familiar quickening of her pulse
began until it roared loudly in her ears, blocking out
everything but the man in front of her. Molly tried to
swallow but found she couldn't. All she could do was
look at him, lost in the depths of his eyes.

"Did you miss me?" His voice was a husky whisper.
Slowly he reached out and lazily stroked her cheek.

"Yes," she whispered.

Jonathan eyed the corner of her mouth, and Molly
gave in to the feelings swirling through her. She tilted
her head back and closed her eyes in anticipation. His
lips devoured hers, seeking and demanding a response.
With a sighing moan, Molly leaned into him and wound
her arms around his neck, not caring that they were

standing in the middle of town, kissing in broad daylight.

He pulled his mouth from hers all too soon, then dropped an arm around her shoulder. "Come on, Molly, let's go eat. I'm starved."

So am I, she thought dizzily. So am I. But not for food. Definitely not for food.

The diner was fairly crowded, she noted as the hostess led them to a booth. While Jonathan studied the menu she gazed around the room. Suddenly her eyes grew to the size of billiard balls, and a strangled groan escaped her. *Oh no!* she thought, dropping her head to her hands. *Not here. Not now!*

"Molly? What's wrong?" Jonathan's brows gathered and he studied her anxious face intently.

Molly lifted her head, and her body tensed in irritation as a surge of anger raced through her. Paul Host was in the restaurant! At that moment he caught sight of her and lifted his hand in greeting. She shook her head in disbelief. What on earth was he doing here? And why would he even bother to come over to their table? Surely he didn't think they had anything to talk about.

"Molly, look at me! What is it?" Jonathan's voice had taken on a sense of urgency. "What's wrong?"

She smiled weakly at Jonathan. "Wrong?" she asked a bit too brightly. "What could possibly be wrong?" What could possibly be wrong? her mind echoed darkly. Just because her former fiancé, a man she'd hoped never to set eyes on again, was heading toward their table didn't mean anything was wrong.

What the devil was Paul Host doing here, anyway? She hadn't seen hide nor hair of him since they'd broken up. Now, the man had to show up here! Resentment tensed her body. The man's timing had always been perfect.

"Hello, Molly." Paul's voice jolted her, and she dragged her eyes to his. The man hadn't changed much, she thought, eyeing the limp smile that graced his thin face.

Conflicting emotions tore through her as she watched him standing there perfectly calm like a long-lost friend stopping by for a chat. Only he wasn't a long-lost friend, and she had nothing whatsoever to say to him. At least nothing that a lady could say out loud and in public. How could he simply present himself? Didn't he know how she felt? Maybe the man's memory was short.

"Hello, Paul," she said coolly, wishing he would just go away. She tried to curb the impotent rage that rocked her. What on earth could he possibly want after all this time?

Jonathan cleared his throat, and she looked up at him in surprise. He was watching her and Paul carefully, his eyes shifting from one to the other. She could tell Jonathan was mentally sizing up the other man, not that there was any comparison. Paul was small and blond, with fair skin and nondescript blue eyes. He was a good six inches shorter than Jonathan and nowhere near as handsome.

"How have you been, Molly?" Paul asked quietly.

"Fine," she snapped, trying desperately to keep a measure of civility to her tone. "And you?" Jonathan's head jerked up and he frowned at her. She realized her attempt at civility had failed.

Obviously jittery, Paul shifted from one small foot to the other. "I, um, I've been fine, too." He flashed her another weak smile, and Molly's lips thinned in annoyance. Wonderful, she thought furiously. Now that he's given a report on the state of his health, maybe he'll leave. His boldness infuriated her.

Jonathan looked at her strangely, then stood up and took control of the situation. "I'm Jonathan Kent." He towered over Paul, and when he extended his hand to the smaller man, Molly noted Paul's hand nearly disappeared in Jonathan's.

"Paul Host," the smaller man repeated, turning his head toward Molly, who was sending him silent signals with her eyes. Couldn't he take a hint?

"We were just about to have some dinner, Paul. Care to join us?"

With a murderous glint in her eyes, Molly turned to Paul, mentally urging him to go away, but he ignored her and smiled broadly at Jonathan. "Thank you, but I've already had my dinner." A relieved sigh escaped Molly. Maybe the man could take a hint after all.

"Perhaps a cup of coffee, then?" Jonathan was talking to Paul, but looking at Molly with a quizzical gleam in his eye.

"A cup of coffee does sound good," Paul ventured.

Molly glared at both men. She couldn't believe Jonathan had actually encouraged Paul to stay. And as for Paul—she turned her angry eyes on him—she couldn't believe he would actually have the nerve to sit down and have a cup of coffee!

Grudgingly she slid over to make room for him, aware that Jonathan was watching her every move intently. Let him be curious, she thought darkly. She wasn't about to start explaining.

Much to her dismay, Paul made himself comfortable. "So, you're a friend of Molly's." He spoke directly to Jonathan, totally ignoring Molly. Fury bubbled through her veins. How dare he speak about her as if she weren't even there!

"Yes, Paul," she returned recklessly, before Jonathan could even open his mouth. "Jonathan is a friend of mine. I have *lots* of friends." Her voice dripped with sarcasm, but if Paul noticed he gave no indication as he turned to give her another smile.

For the first time, Molly noticed how weak his chin was. Lord, she wondered, how on earth could she have ever imagined herself in love with him? To think she had almost agreed to spend the rest of her life with this insensitive, uncaring man. The thought caused a shudder. She couldn't even stand the thought of spending the next few minutes with him, let alone a lifetime.

"Molly?" Paul waited until she looked at him. "How's your aunt?"

In an effort at self-control Molly took a deep breath and counted to ten. How dare he even ask about her aunt? The only thing Paul cared about was himself. She didn't answer him, fearing nothing civil would roll off her tongue.

"Molly?" He reached out and touched her arm, and she instinctively recoiled. His touch was cold and clammy and set her nerves on edge. "I hope you know that what happened . . . well . . ." He shrugged. "It was probably for the best. I like your aunt. I really do. But, under the circumstances, I just felt it best—"

She didn't want to hear any more, didn't want to listen to his weak excuses. The only thing she wanted was for him to leave. And now. "Paul, it was nice to see you again. Sorry you have to go so soon."

He looked at her in surprise. But, seeing the dark glint in her eyes, the man blessedly got the message. He shook his head slowly and pulled himself reluctantly to his feet. "Yes, it's probably best if I get going. Nice to meet you, Jonathan." He gave her one last look before scurrying away.

Molly glared at his retreating back for a moment, then closed her eyes and let her anger dissipate. Why today of all days did he have to wander back into her life? Even for just a moment?

Breathing easier, Molly began to relax. Then her eyes fell on Jonathan. Uh oh, she thought, eyeing the curious look on his face. Here it comes.

"That was some performance, Molly." Jonathan leaned back against the booth and surveyed her quizzically. There was a hint of a smile on his lips.

"What do you mean?" she replied innocently.

"Ever since you spotted that Paul character, you've been acting very strange."

Tension coiled like a snake inside her, but Molly did her best to act nonchalant. "Strange? I don't think I've been acting strange at all," she returned breezily.

"Who is that guy, Molly?"

"What guy?"

"Paul."

She shrugged nonchalantly. "Oh, just a man I know. He used to be the administrator at my school." That wasn't a lie. Paul had been the administrator, that's how they'd met. Luckily, after their wedding was called off, Paul had requested a transfer and got it.

"Why did you get so angry when he sat down? Is he the mystery man from your past?"

Stunned, Molly's gaze flew to his. Her mouth snapped shut, and she glared at Jonathan. "Angry? Me? I don't know what you mean. I wasn't—"

"Is he, Molly?"

Couldn't Jonathan Kent be just a little less persistent just once in his life? she wondered miserably, cursing Paul Host. "I'm starved," she announced. "Let's eat." She grabbed the menu from behind the sugar jar and began reading. "Special today is meat loaf. You haven't lived until you've had the diner's meat loaf. Loaded with home-cooked gravy and a giant dollop of mashed potatoes on the side. It's heavenly." She fairly swooned.

"Molly?" Jonathan's voice had taken on an ominous tone. He reached out and tugged her hand, trying to get her to look at him, but she refused.

"Unless of course, you'd rather have the corned beef with boiled potatoes," she rattled on. "It's good, too. But personally, Jonathan, I think I prefer the meat loaf."

"All right. That's it!" Jonathan grabbed her hand and hauled her to her feet in one swift motion.

"Jonathan!" she protested. "What are you doing? Where are we going? We haven't even ordered yet." The menu fluttered from her hand.

Ignoring her protests, Jonathan pulled her through the crowded diner.

"Jonathan," she groaned, conscious of all the curious eyes that were now focused on them. "Where are we going?"

"Somewhere we can talk."

"I don't want to talk," she insisted, struggling to pull free of him. But Jonathan only tightened his hold on her hand. "I want to eat."

"Tough!" he snapped over his shoulder.

Molly stopped abruptly, refusing to budge another inch. "Look, Jonathan, I really am starving. Can't this wait?" She implored him with her eyes.

"No, Molly, it can't wait." Jonathan dragged her outside and down the walk, finally stopping about a block away from the diner. "Now, who is he?" There was a stubborn tilt to his chin and Molly knew she wasn't about to get out of this one easily.

"He's just a man, Jonathan," she said wearily.

He dropped his hands to her shoulders. His touch sent a warming shiver skipping down her spine. "Just a man?" His brow lifted skeptically. "Then why did you react like that when he came over?" He tilted her face and forced her to look at him. His features were still and intensely serious.

This is ridiculous, she thought, raising her chin a notch. "Like what!"

Jonathan's fingers claimed her chin again and he absently began stroking her. His touch was meant to be soothing, but it had just the opposite effect, and a slow warmth threatened to engulf her. She tried to step back out of his reach, anxious to break the spell that was slowly encompassing her, but Jonathan's grip on her shoulder tightened.

"Every time I come near you, Molly, you jump like a wounded deer. Why? Is it because of that Paul character?" His soft voice rubbed over her exposed nerves, and she lowered her chin, feeling like a fool. Jonathan was right, of course. Every time he touched her, she did flinch. Not because she was afraid of him, though. But because his touch sent her spinning into regions of desire. Regions she had never ventured into before. Regions that frightened her more than she wanted to admit.

"Molly, please tell me who he is." Jonathan's voice was insistent. And from the determined look on his face, she realized she was going to have to tell him sooner or later.

Oh blast! What difference could it possibly make now? She lifted her chin, took a deep breath and met his gaze. "Paul Host was my fiancé."

Chapter Eight

Jonathan's astonishment was quick and genuine. His brows rose, almost disappearing into the curls that fell across his forehead. "Do you mean to tell me that you and that nervous little man were *engaged*?"

Did he have to make the word sound so distasteful? "Yes, Jonathan." Molly nodded her head and sighed wearily. "I was engaged to that nervous little man."

"I don't believe it." Jonathan shook his head. "Why—how—I mean, what happened?"

Her spirit dragged. The last thing she wanted to do at the moment was waste any more time talking about Paul Host.

"Can't we please just drop it, Jonathan? It's over and done with." She sighed heavily. "Paul Host hasn't been a part of my life for a long, long time. I'd like to keep it that way."

"Did he hurt you?" Jonathan dropped his hands protectively to her shoulders. His fingers dug into her soft flesh as he studied her face. "He hurt you very much, didn't he?" He studied her face carefully for a moment, then swore softly under his breath. "That little—"

"It doesn't really matter Jonathan. It was a mistake to begin with, and a mutual decision to break it off. I don't really want to talk about it." It felt good to have his hands on her shoulders. Good to have him touching her again.

"I do," he stated firmly. "Tell me what happened." Thick lines marred his brow, and his voice shook with an emotion she couldn't identify. "Someday you're going to have to trust someone. Why not me?" The way he said it took her breath away.

"Trust you? Why should I trust you?" she cried, suddenly remembering their argument about his grandmother. He wanted her to trust him, yet he hadn't given her any reason to. Molly stiffened, reinforcing her defenses.

"You should trust me because I care about you. Oh, Molly, I care." His voice was soft as he gathered her reluctant body close.

His words seemed to crumble the last of her resistance. Did she dare believe that Jonathan cared for her? And was she ready to admit how she really felt about him? Despite all her denials, Molly knew Jonathan Kent had the power to hurt her—a hurt she feared might never go away. Sighing, she allowed herself to relax against him. A torrid warmth engulfed her as her body met his, leaving her feeling all too vulnerable.

"I won't hurt you," Jonathan whispered, stroking her hair. "Trust me."

She longed to reach out to him. To hold him. To trust him. But she didn't dare, did she?

"Let's walk, Molly." Sensing her misgivings, Jonathan dropped an arm around her waist and steered her down the sidewalk. She followed his lead, not knowing or caring where he was taking her. She didn't ever want to be hurt again. But she certainly didn't want to hurt Jonathan, either.

He would be gone in a little while. Just the thought was painful. Whether he meant to hurt her or not, when Jonathan left it would be another shaft of pain for her to bear. And she didn't know if she could stand it. She had to get used to the idea that Jonathan Kent was not a permanent fixture in her life. She hated to admit it, but she had gotten used to the idea of having Jonathan around. In just a few days he had driven through her life like a turbulent spring storm, turning her world totally upside down. When she wasn't with him, she missed him, thought about him. When he left, she would be alone again, and she didn't know if she could bear it.

They entered the park and Jonathan led her to a bench near the entrance. The park was deserted except for a few robins that squawked and flew about with reckless abandon.

Pulling her down next to him, Jonathan kept his arm around her shoulders. "Now, from the beginning, Molly, tell me all about this Paul character."

Molly mutely shook her head. Why waste any more time talking about Paul when her heart and mind were filled with Jonathan?

"Molly," Jonathan coaxed, his voice soothing, "maybe I'll be able to understand. You know, you're going to have to trust someone sometime. You certainly can't spend the rest of your life alone."

"I'm not alone," she said fiercely. "I have Aunt Emily."

His eyes were sharp and assessing as they watched her struggle to hold on to her composure. A sudden, dazzling light flickered in his eye and he smiled tenderly. "That's it, isn't it? Paul mentioned something about your aunt. Your breakup had something to do with your aunt, didn't it?"

Molly's lips thinned, and she simply nodded her head, not trusting herself to speak.

"Tell me the whole story from the beginning." It was no longer a question, but a command. He pulled her close until her head rested against his broad shoulder.

Taking a deep breath, Molly plunged in. "I'd known Paul about a year. We'd worked at the same school. We began dating, and after a while we realized that we had a lot in common. When he asked me to marry him, I accepted. He seemed decent and kind." The last few words were said more to reassure herself than to reassure Jonathan.

"Did you love him?"

His question brought a small smile to her lips. "I guess at the time I thought I did. But now I realize I didn't love him at all. Certainly not the way a wife should love her husband. It was more like a companionable friendship."

"Why did you break up?" He gently stroked her shoulder, urging her on, reassuring her of his presence.

"We had agreed that Aunt Emily could live with us after we were married. She's always been a part of my life, Jonathan," she cried, her voice trembling with anger. "Aunt Emily raised me. I wanted her to live with us." Just talking about it made her fury grow.

"But that Paul character didn't?"

Molly nodded furiously, and Jonathan muttered something under his breath. "At first Paul agreed. He thought it was a fine idea. Then a few months before the wedding he took me to see this place on the outskirts of town. He wanted me to put Aunt Emily away in some wretched rest home." Her eyes filled with sudden tears and Jonathan bent to wipe them away, replacing them with tiny kisses.

"Go on," he urged, tightening his arms around her until Molly felt warm and protected. She took a deep, shuddering breath.

"When I told him it was out of the question, Paul said I had to make a choice: either him or Aunt Emily." Molly sniffled, then wiped her nose on the handkerchief Jonathan produced.

"Is that when you broke it off?"

Molly nodded. "I wasn't about to put Aunt Emily away somewhere just for his convenience."

"Good for you, Molly girl." He was silent for a moment, and Molly snuggled closer to him, relieved that the entire story was finally out in the open. The soft rhythm of his breathing soothed her as she buried her face closer to the soft pad of his shoulder.

"Oh my God!" Jonathan suddenly bolted upright and held her at arm's length.

Startled, Molly stared at him in confusion. "Jonathan, what is it?"

"That's it, isn't it? That's why you got so upset about my grandmother." Grinning, he shook his head. "Now I understand. You thought I was going to do to my grandmother what Paul wanted to do to your aunt! No wonder you were acting like I was an ax murderer out on a three-day pass. Poor Molly," he crooned softly. "Listen to me." He drew back and forced her chin up.

His eyes bore into hers until she felt she was drowning. "You have to believe me when I tell you that I would never do anything like that to my grandmother. I'm *not* Paul Host. And I'm not at all like him. I would never do anything to hurt my grandmother, Molly. I love her." His eyes softened as they tenderly met hers. "I want you to trust me, Molly."

Eyes wide, she stared at him. Her eyes lovingly traced his features. Did she dare? she wondered. Surrendering to a force stronger than her will, Molly closed her eyes. Maybe it was time for her to trust again. To risk everything. She took a deep breath.

"All right, Jonathan," she said softly, reaching up to caress his cheek. "But you have to help me. You want me to trust you, but—can you understand how I have doubts?" She looked up at him expectantly. "Your grandmother—"

Jonathan chuckled softly. "Molly if you know my grandmother, you know how stubborn she can be. Not to mention independent, headstrong and hardheaded. Just like your aunt." Molly smiled and nodded her agreement. "Grandmother asked me to come home to help her iron out some problems. Nothing more. Nothing less. Honest." He gave her a reassuring smile, and Molly realized she believed him. "Your aunt trusts me. Don't you think you can at least try?"

Molly looked at him. His eyes were so tender that it warmed her heart. Jonathan was asking her to trust him without really giving her a reason to. Could she do it?

Silently she stared at him. She studied the angles of his handsome features. His face spoke of tenderness. His eyes of honesty and integrity. No, he wasn't Paul Host. He would never be that kind of man. Jonathan

Kent was too kind, too warm. Jonathan Kent was one of a kind.

Euphoria swept through her, filling her heart, and all at once, she knew. In her heart. In her mind. And with every ounce of her being. She had to trust him. She was in love with him. She loved Jonathan Kent!

Molly took a deep breath. "Jonathan," she said softly, "I trust you."

He gave a delighted whoop and scooped her up into his arms, settling her on his lap. "I won't ever hurt you, Molly girl," he whispered. "Promise."

His words swept away every ounce of doubt. She slid her arms around his neck and lifted her face for his kiss. It seemed like an eternity until his lips closed over hers. Basking in the newness of her feelings and in the heady sense of trust that she had found again, Molly responded to him like someone who'd been lost in the desert. She drank in his lips, savoring the taste of him with an intensity that frightened her. A whimper of desire escaped her, and Jonathan drew back hesitantly.

"Molly?" His eyes met hers and she moaned softly.

"Oh, Jonathan." She wound her fingers into the soft silk of his hair as he laid his cheek against hers. Intoxicated by love, she inhaled deeply and raised a hand to hesitantly trace the contours of his face, awed by the beauty of him.

She realized that until that moment, she had never truly known love. Sanity fled as she eagerly lifted her mouth, twining her arms tightly around his neck. She was hungry for his kiss, for his caresses.

"Oh, Molly girl," he whispered, "trust me. You won't be sorry." His words freed the last bits of restraints around her heart, and she surrendered her will completely to Jonathan.

Love. Trust. She'd never realized how wonderful the words were until now. She loved Jonathan. Trusted him.

Her skin tingled with anticipation as his lips wove a path down her cheek and across her face. His touch was as light as a feather, and her body obeyed the new command. She turned her mouth toward his, no longer able to bear the absence. Jonathan's mouth found hers, and a whimper of pleasure sounded deep in her throat as his warm fingers slid slowly up her back, coming to rest on the soft curve of her breast. She sipped at his lips gratefully, taking what he offered and longing desperately for more. His parted lips devoured hers, seeking and demanding a response. His tongue parted her lips, exploring the honeyed recesses of her eager mouth. A wispy cloud of passion muddled her thoughts as she leaned closer to him, her body ignited by the warmth of his.

"Molly—" his lips left hers to nuzzle her earlobe "—I'm a grown man, and necking in the middle of a public park in broad daylight, knowing that half the town is probably watching, is not my idea of fun. Not that I care, mind you," he added, sliding his mouth back down for another kiss.

With a wanton smile, Molly lifted her arms and pulled him closer, not wanting to relinquish the fresh pleasures he aroused. Her lips parted under his and her fingers slid through the silky tangle of his hair as her breathing grew ragged.

"Molly," he groaned huskily, reluctantly pulling away, "what we need is some privacy. Unless we get over to the village hall pretty soon, I'm afraid we might do something to scandalize the whole town." His tone of voice made her laugh, and she arched closer to him for one last kiss, her body tingling with flagrant desire.

"You're right, Jonathan," she agreed at last, slowly unwinding her arms. Reluctantly she slid off his lap and wiped a trace of lipstick from his mouth.

Running a hand through his hair, Jonathan glanced around. "Cyanide Simpson is probably having a field day." He looked at her tenderly. "We have so little time left, Molly. I don't want to spend it under the watchful eye of the whole town." His voice had dropped to a seductive whisper that sent a tingle down to her toes.

"Jonathan Kent! Whatever do you have in mind?" Her eyes twinkled. "I'll have you know that as 'Miss Emily's poor spinster niece' I have a certain reputation to maintain." She gave him her severest frown and Jonathan chuckled.

"Yes, I know." He dipped his head for another quick kiss. "Let's see what we can do to change that," he growled wickedly, grabbing her hand and pulling her to her feet. "*After* we check out the senior center."

A half hour later they stood in the mayor's office.

"Are you sure this is all there is?" Jonathan's brows knitted together as his eyes scanned the sheaf of papers the mayor had given to him. Molly peeked over his shoulder, trying to get a glimpse of the papers.

"Afraid so, Mr. Kent." Mayor Taylor leaned back in his chair and pushed his glasses up higher on the bridge of his nose. "That parcel of land was one of the founding plots of Hillchester. After the last descendent of Chester Hill, the town's founder, passed on, that property was put up for sale. Some big corporation bought it." The mayor paused to scratch his bald head and adjust his feet atop his desk. "The senior center was already built by then. Think one of Chester's grandkids had it built, but that was before my time." The mayor smiled pleasantly.

"Who was the attorney that handled the estate sale?" Jonathan was shuffling through the papers again, and Molly watched him carefully.

The mayor thought for a moment. "Harry Peals, I believe."

"Know where I can find him?" Jonathan inquired politely.

The mayor chuckled softly. "Hillchester Cemetery. Harry passed on a while back. About ten years ago, wasn't it, Molly?"

Molly shook her head. "I'm sorry, Mayor. I don't remember exactly when it was."

Mayor Taylor's bushy white brows drew together and he sat up abruptly, letting his feet drop to the floor with a thud. "Son, do you think there was something wrong with the transaction?" The mayor looked genuinely concerned, and there was a moment of taut silence. A big bear of a man, Franklin Taylor had been the mayor of Hillchester for as long as Molly could remember. He was, Molly thought, the most unlikely candidate for politics. Soft-spoken and deliberately polite, he ran the business of the town with a cool efficiency that astounded his few political adversaries. There had been some talk that this would be his last term as mayor, but Molly couldn't imagine anyone else handling the job. If there was any hint of something gone amiss, he would do everything in his power to right it. Franklin Taylor was a fair and decent man.

Jonathan shook his head and smiled. "No, I don't think so. Everything here looks in order. Just thought I might learn a little more from the attorney himself."

The mayor's relieved sigh filtered through the cramped office. "Glad to hear it, Mr. Kent. Wish I could tell you more, but you've got everything there." He nodded his head toward the papers Jonathan held in his hand. "You know, I can't remember the last time the townsfolk were divided over an issue the way they are over this property." Mayor Taylor grinned broadly. "Guess it's good, though—shows people still care what happens in this town."

Jonathan smiled politely. "Do you have any idea how many code violations the center's been cited for?"

The mayor leaned back in his worn leather chair again. "You'd have to check directly with the zoning board, but I'd guess probably eight to ten. The board wouldn't have ordered the building shut down if there was just a few minor problems. New owners were properly notified of the violations. The official letters are in with those papers. They were given ample time to correct the problems before we closed the place down. But I guess they decided the place wasn't worth investing so much time and money. That's when they petitioned for a zone change." The mayor turned his attention to Molly.

"I'm sorry all this has upset Miss Emily. We had no choice in the matter. Once the owners refused to correct the problems, we had to shut the place down for the public's safety."

Molly smiled at his thoughtful expression. She had always suspected that the mayor had a soft spot for her aunt.

After giving the papers another cursory glance, Jonathan handed them back to the mayor. "Thank you for your time, Mayor Taylor. I think I have everything we need." Molly looked at him in surprise. Had Jonathan discovered something that might help the center? Her spirit soared with sudden hope.

The mayor stood up and offered Jonathan his hand. "Glad to help, son. I suspect we'll be seeing you around for a while." He smiled affectionately at Molly and gave her a broad wink. No doubt the gossip mill had found its way to the mayor's office.

Jonathan returned the mayor's smile and shook his hand.

"Give Miss Emily my regards, Molly."

She smiled. "I will, Mayor."

Jonathan cupped her elbow and ushered her out of the room.

"Jonathan," she asked breathlessly, trying to keep up with him as he hurried down the stairs. "Did you find anything out?"

"Nothing out of the ordinary. All the papers seem in order."

Molly stopped abruptly and her hope dimmed. "Then what are we going to do?"

Jonathan grinned and grabbed her hand. "Come on, I'll show you."

Chapter Nine

Jonathan!" Molly gasped. "What on earth are you doing?" Her voice cut through the still night air as she watched him loosening the board that had securely barricaded the front door to the senior center.

"Jonathan?"

She inched closer to him and grabbed a handful of his shirt as her worried gaze swept the street. It was dark and deserted at this hour. A worried frown pulled at her mouth. First, Aunt Emily had gotten arrested for picketing in front of the senior center. Now, Miss Emily's "poor spinster niece" was breaking into the place! Molly shook her head. If word got out—

"Relax, Molly," Jonathan teased, pulling the board off and giving the door a shove, "I know a good attorney."

With an eerie creak, the door slowly opened. Molly's eyes widened, and she coughed as a rush of hot, stale air licked her face.

Waving the musty air in front of them, Jonathan hesitantly took a step inside. "How long has this place been closed down?" he whispered.

"A few months."

She clutched his shirt tighter and peeked around him. Her pulse quickened. "Jonathan? I—I don't know about this."

"Trust me, Molly." He reached around and circled her waist with his arm, pulling her inside with him. The aged wood floor groaned under their weight, and Molly snuggled closer to Jonathan, grateful for his warmth and the security of his arm.

The senior center was eerie in the dark, and a shiver of fear raced up her spine as her eyes struggled to adjust to the darkness.

"Are you cold?" A solitary shaft of moonlight filtered in through one of the upper windows. The light danced across the planes and angles of Jonathan's face. His eyes met hers in the darkness, and her heart began to flutter wildly.

Molly shook her head and burrowed closer to him. "No, I'm not cold."

"Scared?"

"I'm not scared," she protested, her voice shaky. "I'm terrified."

"Molly." He laughed and slid his other arm around her waist, gathering her close until his body warmed hers. "Don't be afraid," he said softly. "I wouldn't let anything happen to you."

With an inward sigh, she laid her head against his shoulder and tried to relax. When Jonathan had suggested they go over to the center and inspect the place, she had readily agreed. She had never dreamed the place would be spooky. What a difference a few months had made!

The darkness wrapped around her like a warm blanket, magnifying her senses. There was an unnatural stillness in the air. The pungent aroma of dampness and dust assaulted her nose, and her eyes burned from the stagnant air. Eerie scratches within the walls announced the residency of rodents. Molly could only hope they were friendly rodents.

Jonathan lifted a hand to stroke her hair. "We won't stay long. I promise. I just want to have a look around. Those papers we found at the village hall sure didn't tell us very much. I wanted to see the place for myself. All right?"

Molly lifted her head. She'd said she trusted him. Nodding, she looked around the room. Her eyes were slowly adjusting to the darkness. "What are we looking for?"

Jonathan slowly inched forward, and Molly's fingers tightened around his waist as she followed his lead.

"I don't know yet." The sigh he expelled was hardly comforting. "Molly, this place is a disaster. No wonder it was closed down."

"It does look pretty dismal," she admitted reluctantly.

"It would help if we had some light."

"The utilities cut off the electricity after the center was closed, but I've got a small flashlight on my key ring." Molly fished in her pocket for her keys and handed them to Jonathan. The penlight cast a small beam across the large empty room.

Funny, she'd never noticed before how dilapidated the center was. The last time she had been there, it had been broad daylight and the center had been filled with people. Streaks of dust now hung from the rafters. The paint was cracked and chipped in places, and old water marks stained the woodwork. A few of the windows were broken, and jagged pieces of glass sat adrift in the panes.

Jonathan moved slowly around the room, with Molly right on his heels. "Oh, Molly," he muttered finally, shaking his head in dismay.

She didn't like the tone of his voice or the sighs that kept slipping from his lips. Aunt Emily had been so certain that Jonathan would be able to help them save the center. But now, after Molly had seen the place for herself, she wasn't so sure. Maybe it just looked worse in the dark, and having been boarded up and neglected for months certainly hadn't helped. "Jonathan, what do you think? Will we be able to save it?"

He shook his head again. "I don't know Molly. I'm not an architect. I'm sure some of the problems are surface. It's the structure I'm concerned about. Not to mention the electrical system and the heating."

Molly's spirits sank. Even if they did manage to scrape up enough money to fix everything—that is, if everything *could* be fixed—there was no guarantee that the zoning commission would vote to keep the shopping center out. If the situation seemed dismal before, now it looked almost impossible. What was she going to tell her aunt? The thought brought a sudden bout of sadness.

"Oh, Jonathan." Her voice trailed off as unshed tears filled her eyes. "Aunt Emily—"

"Molly—" turning her around to face him, he slipped an arm around her waist "—this place is a lot worse than I expected, but it's not totally hopeless. Not yet, anyway. I've got a friend who's an architect. I'll give him a call and see if he can get out here to look the place over. We've still got almost a week before the town meeting." He cupped her chin and smiled. "Now don't worry. We'll work something out."

Looking up at him, Molly's heart tripped over its own beat. Her eyes traced his face. She didn't need any light; she knew every plane, every angle of his features. Her breathing grew ragged as he lifted one hand to brush a strand of hair from her face.

"Do you know what we have here?" Jonathan's voice had taken on a husky whisper, and Molly shook her head, unable to take her eyes from his.

"A disaster?" she whispered, feeling a sudden lurch of excitement deep in her heart.

"Privacy," he whispered softly. Reaching his other arm around her, he pulled her closer. "Absolute, total privacy. Listen." His words were as soft as a caress, and icy shivers of delight raced up and down her spine.

Closing her eyes, she relaxed against him. The only sound she heard was the rapid thudding of her heart beating within her chest.

"Do you hear it, Molly?" She could hear the smile in his voice. "There's no one here but you and me. No cats. No kids. Not even Cyanide Simpson."

Jonathan cupped her face with his hands. His lips weaved a sensuous path across her skin as he planted soft kisses across her upturned face.

Her legs seemed to melt, and she sagged against him. "Jonathan," she whispered huskily, struggling to control the feelings that were making her reel.

"Oh, Molly," he groaned, tightening his arms until she was pressed against him from shoulder to thigh. Heated by his warmth, she arched her body closer,

molding herself to him as her arms slid around his neck.
Her fingers wound through the silky depths of his hair.

She lifted her mouth hungrily, waiting for his kiss.
Her senses catapulted as his mouth claimed hers with an
intensity that dropped the floor from beneath her.

"Jonathan," she moaned, gasping for air. His sweet
tongue dipped and darted between her parted mouth as
his hands roamed her back, setting her skin aflame
through the thin material of her dress. His hands scaled
the length of her, down the gentle sloping curve of her
hips, cupping her bottom to bring her closer until she
felt the brand of him everywhere he touched. Her heart
took a perilous leap, and her nerves danced from the
explosive currents that raced through her.

She touched her tongue to his, shyly at first, then with
wicked abandonment as wild desire intoxicated her. She
relished the exquisite texture of him, the wondrous taste
of him. Kissing him back, she hungrily took what he
offered, wanting more.

"Molly." Her name came out a husky groan as Jonathan slid his mouth from hers. She could feel his warm
breath mingle with her own as his lips traced a sizzling
path over her cheeks and her brows. Lazily his mouth
wandered downward, and she pressed closer to him as
he bent to nuzzle her ear.

A fiery blaze swelled inside her, and Molly gasped,
pulling his mouth back to her own. His kiss deepened
as his hand slid up to the curve of her breast, seeking,
searching. Jonathan's touch was warm, his fingers sure
as they slid across the thin cloth of her dress to find the
buttons.

With delicate ease, he pushed the material free, and
she shuddered at the touch of his hand against her bare
skin. With deliberate care, he took possession of her

mouth and body. His fingers caressed her breast as tenderly as his mouth caressed her lips.

She grew dizzy, engulfed in darkness and desire. Her small moan of pleasure was muffled as cravings as ancient as time took hold.

Her hands moved slowly, roaming and exploring his wide shoulders, the muscled contours of his back. She wanted to protest when he pulled his lips from hers, but no words came out, just a hasty puff of breath as his lips slid past her chin to nestle in the bed of her neck.

Trapped in a tangled web of desire, ecstasy and pleasure, Molly tried to push away the nagging fear that filtered through her hazy thoughts.

Jonathan was here now, but what would happen when he left? A chill washed over her, and she tightened her arms around him, trying to ward off the echo of reason. She loved him. The realization was still new, still fresh. She belonged to Jonathan. All her life, she knew, she had waited for this magic moment. But what would happen when he left? Tears stung the back of her eyelids. Molly forced her mind to go blank. Reason and sanity fled as need pummeled her. Jonathan was here now. And she loved him. Oh, how she loved him.

Her head fell back as his mouth inched downward across the hollows of her throat, down the creamy expanse of her breast. His tongue flicked her nerves awake until she nearly screamed with desire. As she drifted in a sea of raging pleasure, the light touch of his tongue against the swollen peak of her breast caused another moan of pleasure to break free from her throat.

"Jonathan." Molly barely recognized the husky voice as her own. Her mouth ached for his and she raised his head, pulling hungrily at his mouth with hers.

"Molly," he murmured against her lips, "I—" Jonathan stopped abruptly as a loud thud echoed through the abandoned building.

"All right! I know you're in there. This is the deputy sheriff. Come out with your hands up!" There was a thump at the door, and Molly froze. She felt Jonathan stiffen in her arms. He slid his mouth from hers and swore softly.

Horror washed over her, and she jumped back out of his arms, hastily pulling her clothing together. She took several deep breaths, trying to slow her breathing. Self-consciously she lifted a shaky hand to smooth her tousled hair.

"I'm going to kill him!" Jonathan muttered.

Her gaze met his in the semidarkness. His eyes were clouded with desire. His mouth still soft and wet from her own. A trace of lipstick stained his cheek, and she reached out a hand to wipe it away.

"So much for privacy," he murmured, capturing her hand and pressing it to his lips. His touch set off another wave of pleasure, and Molly gave herself a mental shake. She had to get a hold of herself and she couldn't very well do it if Jonathan was touching her. She reluctantly pulled her hand free and mentally cursed Junior.

"Miss Molly, is that you?" Junior's flashlight found her face, and she blinked against the sudden brightness, lifting her hand to shield her eyes. "You all right? Who's that with you?" Junior did his best to sound threatening, but his voice shook with fear. He stepped into the room, letting the beam of his flashlight find Jonathan.

"It's me, Junior," Jonathan said with a frustrated sigh. "And Miss Molly is fine."

"Mr. Kent, whatcha doing here this time of night?"

Jonathan turned to Molly, a mischievous gleam in his eye. Molly's breath caught. He wouldn't. Would he? "We were—"

"Junior," Molly interrupted before Jonathan could finish. "Jonathan and I were..." Her voice trailed off, and she looked helplessly at Jonathan, suddenly lost for words. Good Lord, what on earth *was* she going to tell Junior?

"Doing research," Jonathan supplied, quickly coming to the rescue. "Miss Molly and I were doing research."

Molly exhaled a relieved sigh as Jonathan slid his arm around her waist, letting his hand come to rest comfortably on her hip. She tried not to squirm as his fingers walked up and down the curve, spreading a fiery warmth through her already-shaken limbs.

"Yes, that's right, Junior," she echoed, nodding her head in agreement. "Research."

Junior scratched his head. "Funny kind of research in the dark."

Jonathan muttered under his breath, and Molly gave him a nudge with her elbow, trying not to smile.

"Junior—" Jonathan's voice was a hushed whisper "—may I tell you something in confidence?"

Junior's head bobbed up and down, and he licked his lips in anticipation. He was onto something.

"I'm working on a case. As a fellow officer of the court, I'm sure you realize how valuable research is in order to present a good defense." Jonathan's voice was the essence of propriety. Only the teasing strokes of his fingers revealed his true feelings. "I haven't lived here in a long time, and Miss Molly offered to personally show me the senior center so that I could have a first-

hand look at the place," he explained helpfully, letting
his fingers trace a delicate little pattern. "We didn't
think you'd mind."

It's a good thing it's dark in here, Molly thought,
fighting back a wicked smile and playfully slapping at
Jonathan's hand.

Junior scratched his chin. "Guess it's all right.
You about through here, though? If the sheriff finds
out—"

"We're through. For tonight. We may have to come
back, though. We didn't quite finish, did we, Molly?"
He turned to her and gave her a long, loving look that
took her breath away.

"No," she said softly, leaning against him. "We
haven't quite finished."

"You can come back if you want to, but personally,
this place gives me the willies." Junior shuddered. "I
wouldn't want to be here all alone."

"We would," Jonathan muttered under his breath as
he hustled her toward the door. "We appreciate your
help, Junior. You can go ahead and close up the place
now."

"Good night, Miss Molly." Junior's voice sounded
wistful.

"Good night, Junior," she called over her shoulder
as they started down the walk.

"You come back any time you need to. Hear, Jonathan?" Junior called after them. "If I can help, you just
holler. Always happy to lend a hand to a fellow officer
of the court."

"Just what we need," Jonathan moaned as he
quickly pulled her down the street. "More help."

Molly tried not to laugh. Junior meant well. He really
did. She slowed her pace and frowned, suddenly re-

membering why they had gone to the center in the first place. "Jonathan? What do you really think about the center? Do you think you can save it?"

Jonathan came to an abrupt stop and pulled her into his arms. "Like I told Junior, we're not quite finished," he growled huskily. "It's my expert legal opinion that this case needs a lot of research, Molly. Private research," he added, giving her a wicked smile.

"Junior would be happy to help," she teased, linking her arms around his waist.

Jonathan groaned softly and she smiled. "Somehow, Molly, I can't imagine myself doing private research with Junior. He's really not my type. Besides, it just wouldn't be the same." Jonathan grinned and dropped a kiss on her nose. "I believe you and I made a deal. You agreed to help with the center in exchange for canceling the debt you owe. Now, don't tell me you don't remember." His tone was properly shocked and Molly lifted her mouth for his kiss. The only thing she remembered at the moment was the feel of his arms around her and the taste of his mouth on hers.

She leaned into him and tightened her arms around him. Private research, Molly thought dreamily as Jonathan's lips covered hers. Sounded like a good idea to her. A very good idea.

Chapter Ten

Molly groaned softly and wearily dragged herself up the stairs, forcing one foot in front of the other. She was dead tired, and every bone in her body ached. The only thing that kept her going was the fact that in just a few short hours she would see Jonathan again. Jonathan. His name brought a smile to her lips. In just seven days, one short week, how her life had changed.

Fumbling for her keys, she unlocked the door and threw it open, dropping her purse to the floor with a thud. With a heavy sigh of relief she slammed the door behind her and rested her weight against it. Lord, what a day!

Emily walked into the foyer, wiping her hands on her apron. She scanned the length of Molly and frowned. "Molly, what on earth happened to you? You're a mess." Emily wrinkled her nose in dismay and waved the air around her. "And you stink."

"Monkeys," Molly stated, pushing back her wet hair.

"Monkeys?" Emily's frown deepened as she took a step closer.

"Field trip," Molly groaned as she rubbed her aching back. Days like this she wished she had gone into a different profession. Something safe and calm, like skydiving.

"Why on earth would you want to take monkeys on a field trip?" Emily pursed her lips and shook her head, causing her cap of silver curls to fly in every direction.

"Aunt Emily—" Molly chuckled softly "—I didn't take the monkeys on the field trip. I took the children." Molly groaned. "Although, I probably would have had better luck with the monkeys. Maybe they would have been better behaved."

Emily sighed and patted her hair. "Molly, don't talk in riddles. At my age, I don't have time to figure them out."

Bending to pick up her shoes, Molly caught a whiff of herself. Her nose wrinkled in dismay. "We went to the zoo," she explained. "Little Darryl got lost. He made a wrong turn coming out of the bathroom and got swept away with a crowd from another school. It took us nearly an hour to find him, and when we did he was—"

"By the monkey cage," Emily finished for her. "Isn't Darryl one of Ralph's grandchildren?" Molly could barely manage a nod. "Must run in the family," Emily commented, giving Molly a soothing pat. "The last year I had his father Clarence in my class, he tried to jump into one of the fish tanks at the aquarium." Emily chuckled softly. "I don't know who was more scared, me or the fish."

Molly nodded. Clarence's escapades as a child were almost as well known as his son's Darryl. It probably did run in the family.

"You'd better go soak in a hot tub now, dear. And give me your clothes. I'll air them out." She took a step closer and wrinkled her nose again. "Maybe I ought to air you out, too."

Molly lifted her damp blouse to her nose and chuckled softly. "I guess I do smell pretty awful. On second thought, maybe we ought to just give these things a proper burial."

"How was he?"

Molly sighed. She was too tired today to try to follow her aunt's thought patterns. "Who?"

"Darryl."

Molly scowled. "That child has a way of always getting into mischief. Lucky thing I found him when I did." Molly shook her head in dismay. "It never fails, Aunt Emily. Every time we take that child on a field trip, he manages to get into mischief."

"Jonathan called, dear."

Her spirits soared at the mention of Jonathan. "What did he have to say? Am I supposed to call him back?" Molly moved through the house, stripping off her clothes. Her aunt reached out two fingers and delicately plucked the articles from Molly's hands, carefully holding them at arm's length.

"No, I don't think so. He said he'd call back. He's over at the senior center with an architect friend of his. Been there all day, from what I gathered. Thinks he might have a solution to our problem." Emily smiled and Molly sighed. She wasn't certain anymore there was a solution to the problem. But she hadn't confided that information to her aunt yet. She was still hanging on to a slim knot of hope.

"Knew we could count on that boy," Emily commented, carefully staying a good distance behind Molly as she finished pulling off her clothes.

Molly chose her words carefully. "Aunt Emily, it's not over yet. Even if Jonathan does have a solution to the code violations at the center, we'll still have to raise enough money to fix everything. And don't forget, there's still the zoning commission to deal with." She paused to peel off her socks. "It's not over," she repeated softly.

"Nonsense!" Emily snapped. "If Jonathan says he has a solution, I believe him. He's a good boy."

Boy! Molly smiled as an image of Jonathan in knickers and knee socks fluttered through her mind. Jonathan was definitely not a boy. Of that she was sure. Jonathan was a man. All man.

And dear Aunt Emily was totally enthralled with him. The feeling was mutual. Just the mention of Jonathan's name brought a girlish smile to her aunt's lips. Molly knew the feeling. It happened to her all the time.

Emily gathered the rest of Molly's clothes and tucked them under her arm. "You know, dear, you worry too much. Take your bath now. And don't forget to wash your hair."

Molly's soft laughter floated through her bedroom as she did a little pirouette. "Don't you think I should wear my new perfume for Jonathan?"

Emily looked horrified. "Not unless you want to scare the pants off the man."

That, Molly decided, was quite an interesting idea. A blush crept up her cheeks at her scandalous thought, and she ducked her head to hide her sudden smile. "Not a chance," she returned solemnly.

"Is Jonathan picking us up here, Molly, or are we meeting him at the village hall?"

"Now, Aunt Emily, you know Jonathan is allergic to Nickodemus."

"Don't know why you don't get rid of that cat," Emily sniffed. "Plenty of folks would be willing to take the little beggar."

"Don't start that again, Aunt Emily. You know how I feel about Nickodemus. He stays."

"No need to get sassy, dear." Emily looked thoughtful for a moment. "If Jonathan isn't coming for us, I guess I'll walk over with you." Molly didn't miss the note of regret in her aunt's voice.

"Aunt Emily, you don't have to go with me. Did you have something else planned?"

"Thought I'd walk over with Ralph and Alma. That is, if you don't mind. Don't like leaving you alone, though."

"Of course, I don't mind," Molly assured her. "And you're not leaving me alone. I have Nickodemus," she couldn't resist adding as she picked up the sleeping ball of fur. She cradled the cat against her, and he let out a soft meow. Molly chuckled as the cat jumped from her arms. Evidently he didn't like her new perfume, either.

"Still..." Emily frowned.

"Aunt Emily, is something wrong?" Her aunt had been acting a little peculiar the past few days. Molly had attributed it to her concern over the senior center, but now she wasn't so sure.

"Wrong? What could be wrong, dear?" Emily smiled and Molly felt a twinge of fear skate up her spine. That wide-eyed, innocent look didn't fool her for a moment.

"Aunt Emily, is something bothering you?" She watched her aunt carefully.

"Oh, for Pete's sakes!" Emily exclaimed in exasperation. "You're as bad as Ralph. Such a worrywart. Nothing's wrong, except the smell in here. Now go take your bath, or you'll be late for the meeting."

A frown creased Molly's brow as she padded to the bathroom and turned on the faucet. She had been so wrapped up in Jonathan the past week that she hadn't spent much time at home. Nor had she seen her aunt all that much. But when she had, her aunt had seemed preoccupied.

As the tub filled, Molly liberally splashed bubble bath into the water. After unbraiding her hair and running a brush through the tangled mess, she eased her aching body into the tub and let out a deep sigh. The water coaxed and eased the weariness from her, and she leaned her head back and closed her eyes.

It had been a wonderful week, she decided happily. Since the night they had run into Paul and she told Jonathan the whole story, their relationship had changed.

Jonathan was pretty remarkable, she decided with a smile as she spread a thick layer of soap bubbles up her arm. He was warm, loving, considerate. And, she reminded herself for the hundredth time, trustworthy.

The thought widened her smile, and she closed her eyes again. The steaming water soothed her aching bones, and she felt the tension leave her.

Jonathan. He was never far from her mind, she thought dreamily, stifling a yawn. She had carefully avoided thinking about the fact that he was scheduled

to return to Portland in just a few days. They hadn't
talked about it, at least not openly. They had carefully
avoided the issue. But Molly knew she would have to
face the fact sooner or later. The thought of life without her laughing, red-haired giant brought on a round
of despair. Sinking lower in the water, Molly laid her
head back and closed her eyes, willing the unpleasant
thoughts away. She just couldn't imagine Jonathan
leaving or her life without him. She was almost certain
he felt the same way.

They had spent every single evening together this past
week. Jonathan would pick her up from school, they'd
stop somewhere for dinner and then head for the senior center to do "research." Private research, Molly
thought with a wicked grin. She couldn't believe it was
just going to end. She wouldn't believe it. Something
would come up. She just knew it.

The ringing of the phone broke into her thoughts.
Molly sat up and shook her head. The phone rang again
and she frowned. Where was Aunt Emily? Had she left
already? Grabbing a large terry-cloth towel, Molly
stepped from the tub and hurried to her bedroom,
trailing a stream of water. She grabbed the receiver just
as the phone stopped ringing.

"Hello? Hello?" Molly frowned. Certain it was
Jonathan, she quickly dialed his grandmother's house.
The phone rang eight times before she finally hung up.
If it was Jonathan, he would call back, she reasoned.
After quickly drying off, Molly wrapped another towel
around her wet head and pulled open her closet.

Since meeting Jonathan, she had taken much greater
pains with her appearance. And after raking through
her closet twice, Molly still couldn't decide what to
wear. Sighing in frustration, she closed her eyes, stuck

out her finger and chose the garment she touched. The
dress was yellow cotton, with peasant sleeves that ac-
cented her slender shoulders. The gathered folds of the
bodice draped delicately across her breasts, and the full
skirt fell to her knees and had a shallow ruffle at the
hem. She smiled. It was one of her favorites. She laid it
across her bed and went to dry her hair.

After carefully applying a thin layer of makeup,
Molly pinned her hair up. Studying her reflection, she
frowned. Jonathan preferred her hair down, and as she
gazed at her reflection in the mirror, she realized she
did, too. Quickly she loosened the heavy strands of her
hair and brushed it until it shone.

She slipped her feet into delicate yellow sandals and
sprayed herself with the last of some French perfume
she had received for her birthday. Satisfied with the results, Molly grabbed her handbag and left the house.

The village hall occupied a large stone building that
sat in the center of town. The mayor's office and most
of the town's municipal offices were housed in the same
building.

Climbing the steep stairs, Molly found the building
ablaze with lights. The senior center was a popular place
and most of the town's residents knew that its fate
would be decided at tonight's meeting. The town, she
had learned in the past week, was equally divided on the
issue. Some favored the idea of having a brand-new
shopping mall, while others, like Aunt Emily, who
wanted to save the senior center, were very much op-
posed. It was going to be a very interesting evening.

The building was mobbed, Molly noted, as she
pushed through the group of men standing outside the
room having a last cigarette. She nodded to a few, who

politely tipped their hats and made a path for her. Her eyes darted around until she finally spotted Jonathan in the front of the room. He was deep in conversation with Mayor Taylor and another man, who she didn't recognize. Judging from the look on Jonathan's face, the conversation was serious.

Molly made her way to the front of the room, taking time to chat to a few people. When Jonathan spotted her, he smiled and waved, then pointed to a row of empty seats in the front of the room.

Not wanting to disturb his conversation, Molly slid into her seat. Where was her aunt? she wondered, turning to survey the room. She finally spotted her a few rows back. But Aunt Emily, Ralph and Alma were engaged in conversation and didn't even glance in her direction. She would have preferred that her aunt sit by her, if only for comfort, if the meeting didn't go well.

Turning back, she found Jonathan's eyes on her, and a warm glow inched up her spine.

"Hi," he whispered as he took his seat. He leaned over to peck her cheek. "I had some last-minute things to discuss with the mayor." He flashed her a dazzling smile and brushed a strand of hair from her forehead.

"Aunt Emily said you phoned. Sorry, I got home late from the field trip. One of the children got lost. Did you find out anything new today?"

Jonathan smiled and her heart flipped over. "I think I've figured out how to save the senior center." He nodded toward the front of the room. "We'll talk later, the meeting's about to start."

Franklin Taylor claimed his seat behind the large table. Someone leaned over and adjusted the microphone for him.

"The meeting will now come to order." His voice could barely be heard above the murmur of the crowd. People in the back were still chatting, and he finally resorted to banging his gavel. "This meeting will now come to order," he repeated. "We're gonna be rather informal tonight. The zoning commission will hear from members of the community concerning the senior center that is located on a parcel of land on the west side of Drake Street." He looked up from his prepared text and frowned, causing his wire-rimmed glasses to slide down his nose. "You folks all know where the center's at. No sense wasting time reading all this. The way I see it, the owners of the land want the village to rezone the land to accommodate a new shopping mall. If the zoning board agrees with the owners of the land, the senior center, which has been closed for building code violations, will be torn down." There were boos and catcalls from the back of the room, and Molly didn't have to turn around to know that one of the voices belonged to her aunt.

"Order, now," Mayor Taylor continued, banging the gavel again. "Order, please."

Molly leaned over to whisper in Jonathan's ear. "How do you think the vote will go?"

He shook his head. "I'm not sure," he whispered softly. "Molly?"

Something in his voice made her stomach drop, and she turned to look at him, aware that Junior, who was sitting behind her, was listening attentively. Jonathan was so close that she could see the tiny flecks of blue in his eyes. "What's wrong, Jonathan?"

He dropped an arm around her chair and caressed her shoulder. "I love you, Molly."

"W-what?" she stammered, looking into Jonathan's eyes.

Junior tapped her shoulder. "He said he loves you, Miss Molly," Junior announced in a voice loud enough to be heard by the entire room. Loud laughter spread like measles across the room, and Molly blushed to the tips of her ears.

For once, she didn't care that they were the center of attention, or that the whole town was watching. Jonathan loved her! After giving Junior a look that would have stopped bullets, Molly leaned over and whispered in Jonathan's ear. "I love you, too."

"She loves him, too," Junior announced with a grin to the waiting crowd, which erupted in a loud round of applause.

Molly's eyes glinted like summer lightning and not even the applause or comments that filtered from the back of the room could dim her excitement. Jonathan loved her. A feeling of euphoria swept over her, blocking out everything and everyone except the man sitting next to her.

Mayor Taylor banged his gavel and smiled affectionately. "Unless anyone else has any more love declarations," the mayor said, looking at Molly and Jonathan pointedly, "I'd like to continue our meeting." He began reading from his prepared text again, and Molly found her thoughts drifting. Her heart was soaring, and she reached out and grabbed Jonathan's hand, linking her fingers tightly through his.

"Mr. Jonathan Kent, would you address the commission."

Jonathan gave her hand a gentle squeeze before rising. With a mixture of love and pride, she watched him approach the mayor, glad that Jonathan was on their side.

"Mr. Kent has been over at the senior center all day, examining the property. I believe he has some information that will be of interest to this commission and the members of this community. Even though Mr. Kent has not lived in Hillchester for a long time, I believe his credentials as an attorney and former resident qualify him to testify before this board on this matter. Mr. Kent." Mayor Taylor handed Jonathan the microphone.

Jonathan smiled and Molly's spirits skyrocketed. He loved her. She still couldn't believe it! Willing her racing pulse to a standstill, Molly drew herself up and forced herself to pay attention.

"As the mayor has informed you, I spent the better part of the day over at the senior center, but I wasn't alone. Mr. William Fisher, an architect with the firm of Fisher and Fisher also accompanied me. After reviewing the property in question, Mr. Fisher is of the opinion that the structure of the building is unsound." Jonathan paused as a loud murmur raced through the crowded room, and Molly shifted nervously, not sure which direction Jonathan was going in.

"I must confess that I had hoped that after Mr. Fisher's investigation, we would be able to come up with a concrete solution to the problem. But after learning the results of his findings, I'm afraid I must agree with Mr. Fisher. It's my recommendation that the center be torn down and the land be rezoned for the shopping mall."

Molly's heart came to an abrupt stop as her head jerked up. She met Jonathan's gaze and felt a feeling of despair wash over her. Her head began to throb and unshed tears stung the back of her eyelids. She stared at Jonathan, praying she had heard him wrong. This wasn't possible. It had to be some horrible mistake.

The room was in an uproar, but Molly heard none of it. The world seemed to have stopped spinning the moment Jonathan had made his announcement.

"Order, please!" Mayor Taylor banged his gavel. "I demand order. Now, please! Let the man finish." He hit the table again and the room grew quieter.

"Ladies and gentlemen," Jonathan began again. He was talking to the entire room, but his eyes were on Molly's. She stared at him, her insides reeling. Finally she pulled her eyes away, unable to look at him any longer.

It was then she knew it was true. It had happened again. A knife twisted deep inside of her, and Molly felt a sense of grief overwhelm her. Jonathan had lied to her. He had betrayed her! All this time she'd thought he was going to help them. He'd said he had a solution. This was his solution? To betray her trust? Had he planned to encourage the board to vote for the rezoning all along?

Fierce black rage pummeled her, and it became increasingly hard to breathe. She had been a fool. A blind, trusting, fool. Jonathan had lied to her and deceived her. But worse, he had deceived her aunt. Jonathan Kent was even worse than Paul Host. At least Paul had been honest about what he was.

Good Lord, Aunt Emily! Molly had forgotten all about her. She twisted in her seat and found, to her surprise, that her aunt was listening to Jonathan with rapt attention.

Was everyone going crazy? she wondered, fighting back the dismal pain that sliced through her heart. She tried to breathe, but found her breath had lodged somewhere in her throat. She couldn't stay a minute longer in the room. She had to get out of there!

Molly jumped from her seat and raced up the aisle, pushing through the crowd that stood at the back of the room. Hot salty tears blinded her, but she angrily brushed them away.

"Trust me," Jonathan had said over and over again, and like a fool she had listened to him. How could she have been so foolish? How could she have been so blind?

"I'll never hurt you, Molly." How many times had he told her that? Over and over until the icy wall around her heart had come tumbling down. She had believed him!

Blindly she raced home, desperate for the sanctuary of her house. Within minutes she was there, and she choked back a sob as she took the stairs two at a time. Jamming her key in the front lock, she threw open the door. With a mournful sob, Molly collapsed on the couch, letting the tears come.

Her worst nightmare had come true. She had fallen in love with a gentle giant. And he had broken her heart.

Chapter Eleven

Molly crept from her bed, grateful that the night was finally over. After crying for hours she had finally fallen into bed, drained and exhausted. Sleep had eluded her, though, as her thoughts had continued to torment her.

She had heard Aunt Emily come home, but Molly had pretended to be asleep when her aunt had knocked at her door. She hadn't been up to talking. Not to Aunt Emily. Not to anyone.

A lingering sense of sorrow and despair tracked her as she quickly pulled on a pair of jeans and a white turtleneck. After tucking her hair into a topknot, Molly picked up her tennis shoes and tiptoed from her room. She had no idea where she was going, but she was going somewhere. Anywhere. Just so she wouldn't have to think about Jonathan.

"Going somewhere, dear?"

She had just made it to the front door when her aunt's voice stopped her dead in her tracks.

"I thought I'd go for a walk." She deliberately kept her back to her aunt. Molly didn't want Aunt Emily to see her swollen eyes. Didn't want her to see the pain she was sure was reflected in her eyes.

"Can't walk off your problems, dear," Aunt Emily said softly. "Why don't you tell me what's bothering you?"

Molly whirled. "Aunt Emily! What's bothering me? You were at that meeting last night. Didn't you hear Jonathan say he thought the center should be torn down?"

Emily nodded softly. "Of course, I did, dear. I may be old, but I'm not deaf."

"Then how can you ask me what's bothering me?" Molly stared at her aunt in horror. Absently Molly lifted her hand and rubbed her throbbing temples. Her head was pounding, and from the trend of the conversation, she had a feeling her headache was about to get worse.

"He told the truth, Molly. You can't fault the man for that. He honestly believes the center should be torn down."

The truth. That was a laugh. Jonathan Kent didn't know the first thing about the truth. She shook her head dully. For someone who had her heart set on saving the center, her aunt was suddenly acting very unconcerned about its demise.

"I'm sure he's got a good reason for what he did," Emily continued. "Why don't you give the poor man a chance to explain? I think you owe him that much."

"Owe him? Owe him! Aunt Emily, I don't owe that man anything." How could her aunt stand here and talk about what Molly owed Jonathan after what he had done to her? To them?

"Yes, you do, my dear," Emily said softly, closing the distance between them. "You love him, and he loves you." Molly closed her eyes as she remembered the previous night. Had it just been hours before that she had felt so happy because Jonathan had said he loved her? It had been for such a brief, shining moment. The calm before the storm.

"Aunt Emily," Molly sighed. "Please try to understand how I feel."

"I do, child. But you must also try to understand how Jonathan feels. I'm sure he's hurting, too. You raced out of the meeting last night without even giving the poor man a chance to explain."

"What's to explain?" Molly shrugged her shoulders regretfully. "I know everything I need to know. I trusted Jonathan and he lied to me. He betrayed me. He betrayed *us*." Her voice rose. "Aunt Emily, I don't understand how you can defend the man."

Emily chuckled softly. "I'm not defending him, dear, just trying to get you to listen to reason. Right now, you're hurting too much to think clearly. I once told you that you needed a man in your life. Someone to make your heart sing and your toes curl. Jonathan Kent is that man, Molly. I can see it in your eyes, see it when you talk about him, when you look at him. Don't throw that away, Molly. Love like that doesn't come along too often. Sometimes only once in a lifetime," she finished softly.

Molly blinked rapidly to hold back a flood of tears. Yes, she loved Jonathan with all her heart, but she didn't trust him. He'd lied to her and betrayed her. What good was love without trust?

Jonathan would be leaving in a few days and he would be out of her life for good. Yesterday, that thought threatened to immobilize her; she couldn't possibly imagine life without him. Now, she would almost be relieved when he was gone. Maybe then it wouldn't hurt so much.

"It's no use, Aunt Emily," she said firmly, grabbing a sweater from the front closet. "It's over between us." She swallowed the lump in her throat and pulled on her sweater.

"Molly, wait, I—" Aunt Emily stopped abruptly.

"What? What is it?" Molly sighed. She couldn't bear to talk about Jonathan anymore, certain she wouldn't be able to stop the flood of tears that was threatening to overflow.

"Nothing," her aunt snapped. "It's just I think you're behaving like a pompous ass!"

"Aunt Emily!" Molly gasped, and her eyes rounded in surprise. In all the years she had lived with her aunt, she had never heard her utter anything even close to a profanity.

"Don't go looking so shocked! I learned a word or two in my day. Not that a lady should go around using them, mind you. But this situation calls for something...a little less delicate." Raising her hand, she pointed a finger in Molly's direction. "Jonathan Kent is the best thing that ever happened to you. You're throwing away the entire relationship over some imagined hurt."

"Aunt Emily," Molly protested, "it's not imagined. Don't you understand that Jonathan betrayed me? I trusted him. I thought he was trying to help us. How could he get up in front of the whole town and recommend that the center be torn down? Everyone knows where you and I stand on the issue. You even got yourself arrested over it." The knot inside her stomach tightened. She still couldn't believe that Jonathan had hurt and betrayed and humiliated her.

"What are you going to do, dear?"

Molly heaved a sigh and pushed back her hair. Obviously her aunt hadn't heard a word that she had said. "About what?" she asked with just a hint of impatience.

"Jonathan."

She loved her aunt dearly, but at times, Aunt Emily was hopeless. Molly lifted her chin to a stubborn angle. "There's nothing to do," she said firmly. "It's over." Maybe if she kept saying the words again and again, eventually she'd believe them.

"Nonsense! There's plenty to do. You could march over there right now and tell the man you love him. Give him a chance to explain."

Molly shook her head. "I couldn't possibly do that."

"And why not!" Emily snapped. "It's the truth, isn't it? I love you like my own daughter, Molly, but sometimes I wonder if you have any brains at all. You love him and he loves you. You're going to throw all that away?" Her aunt looked thoroughly appalled. "Do you want to spend the rest of your life alone?"

"I'm not alone," Molly returned softly, forcing down the bitter taste that rose in her mouth. "I have you."

Emily sighed in exasperation. "I'm not going to be around forever, dear."

"Aunt Emily! Don't say that," Molly pleaded. Her aunt seemed full of surprises this morning. First she was cussing. Now she was talking about not being around forever.

"Why not? It's the truth and it's about time you faced facts. Someday I'm gonna be gone. Then what? You want to spend your life with that miserable cat?"

Anguish squeezed Molly's heart. "Aunt Emily, nothing is going to happen to you for a long, long time. Please don't talk like that."

"Molly, you have to face the fact that I'm not always going to be around. You have to think of your own life. A life you should spend with Jonathan."

Molly couldn't respond. She was too busy thinking of all the dreadful things her aunt's words implied. Was it possible her aunt was trying to tell her something? Her mind raced. Aunt Emily hadn't been sick recently. In fact, she had always been in remarkable health, considering her age. Listening to her now, Molly wondered if her aunt was trying to break some news.

"Aunt Emily, are you sure you feel all right? You're not sick, are you?" Her words came out a frightened whisper, and she looked at her aunt anxiously.

"Oh blast, child!" Emily gave an unladylike snort. "Never felt better in my life. I just think it's time for you to start thinking about your own life."

"Are you sure you're feeling all right?" Molly reached out and took her aunt's hand in hers. She loved her so much. She couldn't bear it if anything happened to her. "Does something hurt?"

Emily scowled and muttered something under her breath. "You haven't heard a word I've said, child, have you?" She leveled a hostile gaze on Molly and sighed deeply. "I can see I'm not getting anywhere with you, so I'm not going to waste my breath. You go for your walk. I've got things to do." Emily turned and marched back into her room.

Molly stood there for a moment, contemplating her aunt's words. A senseless trembling rocked her. Was she losing everything she loved? Molly wondered as she opened the door and slipped outside. First she had lost Jonathan. Was she going to lose her aunt, too?

The day was just coming to life as she walked through the familiar streets of the town. It was the same town she had lived in and walked through her whole life, but today it was different. Today, all the color seemed to be gone.

She rounded the corner. The diner was getting ready to open. The front door was propped wide with a brick, and the smell of freshly brewed coffee filtered through the early morning air. Normally Molly would have stopped for a cup, but this morning, just the thought of coffee turned her stomach.

She waved to the owner and hurried on. She didn't want to talk to anyone. Not just yet. She had to sort things out in her mind. Would she ever walk through town again without thinking about Jonathan?

Everything seemed to be a constant reminder. The ice-cream parlor. The diner. The park. Even the sheriff's office. It seemed as if she and Jonathan had gone everywhere together. Would her life ever be the same? Would she ever be able to look at the old familiar places without thinking about him?

The pain deepened, and Molly shuddered, pulling her sweater tighter around her. She walked through town, unaware of where she was going. When she found herself in front of the school, she fished in her pockets for her keys. Spring break was in just a few weeks. Now might be a good time to get a head start on cleaning her room. If she kept busy, maybe she wouldn't have to think. Maybe the hurt would go away.

Molly let herself into the empty building and quickly headed to her classroom. She swung the door open, and a sob tore at her as she remembered the day Jonathan had come to her classroom and had gotten stuck in the chair. Wasn't there anywhere she could go where his memory wouldn't haunt her?

Molly shook the thought from her mind. She couldn't think about that now. It was over. Now she had to get on with her life. And she had work to do.

After donning an apron, she tore into her room, pulling down pictures and washing desks. Tackling her supply closet next, Molly pulled everything out and meticulously assembled it all in perfect order before replacing it. She counted every pair of scissors, every jar of glue, every crayon and every pencil.

With that done, she filled a pail with hot soapy water and began the task of scrubbing her blackboards. The janitor usually took care of that, but today Molly was certain the hard work would soothe her spirit. Once the boards were done, she rolled up the oval braid rug that the children sat on for story time. She'd have it sent to the cleaners first thing on Monday.

Satisfied with the results of her labor, Molly took off her apron and sat down at her desk. With Easter coming, the children would need a special art project to take home. She started several, discarding each one after a few moments. Nothing seemed to satisfy her.

She emptied her desk, then rearranged it twice. She was becoming exhausted. She leaned back in her chair and closed her eyes. At least she had gotten something accomplished. Maybe now she could sleep. It was time to go home.

With a final satisfied look around her room, she let herself out and locked up the building. Fearing she might run into Jonathan, she took a shortcut through the park. Jonathan would be gone in a few days. The thought hammered in her brain. Maybe then her life would go back to normal. No, her mind muttered, her life would never be the same. A gentle giant had stolen her heart and broken it. Somehow she knew she'd never be the same.

The day had grown warm, and Molly peeled off her sweater, tying it neatly around her neck. As she rounded the corner by her house, her eyes widened, and she came to an abrupt stop. What the devil was going on?

Clarence Pritchard's police car was in front of her house. The siren was blaring and the lights flashing. For a moment, she stared, stupefied. It was the town's only police car. Clarence never ran the siren or used the lights except during the Fourth of July Parade. What was happening?

A sudden thought churned her stomach, and she broke into a run, her heart pounding. *Aunt Emily*.

"Clarence!" she called, bounding up to the car. "Clarence?" The car was empty, but the keys were still in the ignition. Where on earth was he?

She tore the outside door open and bolted toward the hall stairs. "Clarence," she screeched, "where are you?"

"Up here, Miss Molly." He called from the top of the stairs.

"Clarence, what's wrong?" she asked as she bounded up the stairs. "Why is the police car in front of the house? And why is the siren on?" She paused to catch her breath. It was then she saw him. He was sitting on the top step, watching her intently. Her heart stopped, weakening her limbs. Jonathan. She took a deep breath. With some effort, she pulled her eyes from his and turned her attention to Clarence.

"He's gone, Miss Molly," Clarence whined, his eyes shining. "He's gone."

"Who's gone?" She was talking to Clarence, but her eyes slid back to Jonathan. He looked wonderful, she thought with a touch of regret.

"Daddy. He's gone." Clarence's voice broke and he hung his head.

Molly looked from one to the other. Jonathan shrugged his shoulders as if to say he didn't know what was going on either.

"Clarence—" Molly touched his shoulder gently "—did something happen to your father?"

"He's gone," Clarence repeated dully, and Molly shook her head. That much she knew.

"Calm down, Clarence." She dug in her pockets and pulled out her keys. Her hands were shaking so much that she couldn't get the door open.

"Let me do it, Molly." Jonathan stood and calmly took the keys from her hands. His fingers brushed hers and her skin tingled. For a moment, their eyes met and that familiar feeling began to grow inside of her. Quickly she turned away from him and patted Clarence's shoulder.

"Let's go inside, Clarence. You can tell me the whole story. From the beginning."

Jonathan swung the door open, and she let out a gasp.

"Jonathan!" she exclaimed as her eyes surveyed the house. Molly stepped inside, her eyes wide. "What the devil is going on, here?" She ran from room to room, her panic growing. The house had been stripped of everything that belonged to her aunt.

Fear quickened her steps, and Molly rushed to her aunt's room. The bed and dresser were still there, but little else. The dresser was stripped clean. All of her aunt's perfumes and lotions were gone, along with the

Irish table scarf that had been on the dresser for as long as Molly could remember.

She rushed to her aunt's closet and yanked the door open. That, too, was empty. All of her aunt's clothes, her shoes and her handbags were gone, too. Even her favorite pillow and quilt were gone.

Fear rose inside her, and Molly tore through the house. "Aunt Emily?" she yelled, her voice growing thin with panic. "Aunt Emily! Where are you?" If this was some kind of joke, it wasn't funny.

After searching every room, Molly finally realized her aunt was not there. Fighting back the fear and hysteria that threatened to break through, she struggled to compose herself. Where was Aunt Emily?

Suddenly she whirled on Clarence, who had been following close on her heels. "Clarence!" Her voice was sharper than she intended. "What on earth is going on?"

Clarence hung his head. "That's what I've been trying to tell you, Miss Molly," he cried. "They're gone!"

Chapter Twelve

Molly grabbed Clarence by the shoulders and gave him a shake. "What do you mean, they're gone? Gone where?" she demanded, her voice rising.

Clarence shifted and stuffed his hands in his pockets. "I don't know. That's why I'm here. Eunice and I went downtown this morning. When we got back, Daddy was gone. All his clothes, everything—gone." Clarence blinked rapidly, and Molly could have sworn the man was going to cry. "Don't know where he could've gone. Or why. Eunice and I love having him around. So do the kids. 'Specially the younger ones. Daddy's got his own room now. Don't have to share no more. Even bought him his own television. Where could he have gone, Miss Molly?"

As upset as she was about her aunt, her heart went out to Clarence. He was as close to his father as she was to her aunt.

"Don't worry, Clarence," she said softly, patting his shoulder. "I'm sure they're all right. We'll find them."

Molly's emotions ran the gamut from rage to fear. Something was going on. For Aunt Emily and Ralph to just disappear without telling anyone was unheard of.

She turned to Jonathan. He was standing quietly behind her. "Do you think something's happened to them?" She spoke quietly so as not to upset Clarence any further, but her voice trembled and she felt weak. Was it fear that made her tremble now? Or Jonathan?

In spite of all that had happened, she had to admit that she felt better knowing he was here. She had seen Jonathan the Attorney in action and felt somewhat comforted by his presence. Remembering the way he had responded the night of Aunt Emily's arrest, Molly knew he could stay calm in a crisis. And this was definitely a crisis.

His eyes met hers, and he smiled wanly. "I don't think so. Come on, I think I might have an idea where they are." He cupped her elbow and led her through the house as she cast a curious eye at him.

"What do you know about this?" Clarence inquired suspiciously as he followed them out to the squad car.

Molly scrambled in back and slid over so that Jonathan could get in. The scent of him assaulted her senses, but she fought it. That relationship was over, she told herself firmly, clutching the back of Clarence's seat as he screeched around the corner, sirens screaming.

"Where to?" Clarence asked, streaking through a red light.

"To the morgue, if you don't slow down," Jonathan told him. "Turn off that darn siren. And the lights, too. We've already caused enough of a disturbance."

"We've created a disturbance!" Clarence wailed. "My daddy's gone!" Clarence repeated, hitting the gas pedal again so that they were thrown back against their seat. "Ain't had a missing person in Lord knows when. And my own daddy yet." He shook his head. "How's it gonna look, me the sheriff and all. Already put out an APB on him."

Jonathan sighed and flashed Molly a weary smile. He looked tired, she thought, eyeing the dark circles that shadowed his face. She noticed he hadn't shaved, either. "Clarence, your father's not missing. Let's just pretend you've misplaced him for the moment." Jonathan ignored Clarence's derisive snort and continued. "Drive over to Maple Street and make a right at the corner. First house on the left."

Molly frowned and turned to Jonathan in confusion. "Who lives there?" she inquired. She remembered the house. It was a large, rambling ranch house that sat nestled on a huge corner lot.

"My grandmother," Jonathan said quietly, leaning his head back against the seat and closing his eyes.

Molly bolted upright. "Your grandmother! Your grandmother lives over on Elm."

"Not anymore," Jonathan commented softly, without opening his eyes.

Molly reached over and touched his shoulder. "What do you mean, 'not anymore'?" she asked, struggling to put the pieces together. Clarence was nearly hysterical. Jonathan was suddenly tight-lipped. Aunt Emily and Ralph had disappeared bag and baggage. And apparently Alma had moved. Molly rubbed her throbbing temples. Was the whole world mad? What was going on?

Jonathan's lids fluttered open, and he rubbed his eyes gingerly. "She moved," he said quietly, turning his gaze on Molly. The look on his face gave her butterflies. He looked so sad that it tugged at her heart.

"Jonathan?" she said softly, unconsciously grabbing his arm. "When did she move?"

"This morning. I helped move her." He settled his head back and closed his eyes again.

Why hadn't he told her his grandmother was moving? she wondered. And what did it have to do with her aunt and Ralph?

She looked at Jonathan. With his eyes closed and the shadow his beard sprinkled across his face he looked so... vulnerable. She reached out and brushed back a copper curl that had fallen across his forehead. He looked so tired. And so very, very sad. Her heart ached.

His eyes opened slowly at her touch and his gaze met hers. "Why did you run out last night?" The look in his eyes was haunting, and Molly pulled her gaze away. She still didn't feel strong enough to look into his eyes. It stirred feelings she didn't want to feel. "You didn't stay to hear the rest of what I had to say." Jonathan's eyes moved slowly across her face, and he sighed regretfully. "You said you'd trust me, Molly," he accused softly.

His words brought another stab of pain, and Molly blinked back the tears. "I—"

"This the place?" Clarence asked as he screeched to a halt.

Jonathan sat up and blinked. "This is it." Wearily he pushed the door open, and Molly scrambled out behind him.

Clarence stood stock still, staring at the building. "You sure this is the place?"

Jonathan sighed. "I'm sure."

Clarence started up the walk. His right hand moved to his holster and he pulled his gun out. "I'm the law here. I'll handle this. Might be some trouble. You civilians stay here."

Jonathan clamped a hand on the man's shoulder. "The only trouble you'll have will be from me if you don't put that damn thing away."

Clarence glanced up at Jonathan, then at Molly. Ralph was right, she decided. Clarence did get carried away at times. Dejectedly Clarence replaced the gun in his holster, but not before giving Jonathan a nasty glare.

"Don't worry, Jonathan," she whispered. "His gun's not loaded. Ralph took his bullets away last year after Clarence nearly shot his foot off." Jonathan rolled his eyes and took her arm as they climbed up the walk.

The house looked deserted, but after Molly rang the doorbell several times, Alma finally answered.

"Hello, children." Alma moved away from the door to allow them to enter. Molly and Clarence volleyed for position as they tried to enter the doorway at the same time.

"Ladies first," Jonathan instructed, clamping a hand on Clarence's shoulder and giving him a tug backward.

Molly stepped into the hallway, with Clarence right on her heels. She took in the freshly painted walls, the bright sunlight streaking in through the clean windows. The place was nice. Homey.

"We were just about to have some tea. Would you children like some?"

"We?" Molly and Clarence caroled in unison. "Is Aunt Emily here?"

"What about my daddy?"

Alma nodded. "They're both here. Come on in."
They followed Alma as she rounded the corner into a
large, bright dining room. Ralph and Aunt Emily were
seated comfortably at a large oak table.

"Aunt Emily!" Molly's voice was pitched high.
"What on earth are you doing here? You scared the life
out of me." She rushed to her aunt and folded her in her
arms, breathing a sigh of relief.

"Daddy, what are you doing?" Clarence stared at his
father.

Ralph stood up and looked at his son quizzically as
Clarence practically collapsed in his arms.

"Quit slobbering on me, boy," Ralph instructed
sternly, holding his son at arm's length.

"Having tea, dear," Emily explained calmly. "Would
you like some? It's fresh. Just brewed it myself." She
smiled sweetly at them.

Molly's temper inched upward. Tea? Tea! Her aunt
wanted to know if Molly wanted some tea? After the
scare she had just had, a tranquilizer would have been
more appropriate. "Aunt Emily, I don't want any tea.
What I want is to know what happened. I've been
looking all over for you. You scared the life out of me."

"Happened?" Emily continued to pour, oblivious to
Ralph and Clarence's animated chatter. "Why, nothing has happened to me. Whatever gave you that idea?"
She flashed Molly a smile, and Molly was sorely
tempted to stamp her foot in frustration. Her aunt was
doing it again. But this time, it wasn't going to work.
She'd just had the scare of her life and she wanted an
explanation. A logical explanation, and right now!

"Why are all your clothes gone, Daddy? You scared
Eunice and me to death," Clarence accused, his face
firmly set in a pout.

"Sit down, boy." Ralph yanked out a chair, and scowled at his son. Clarence dropped heavily into the chair and wearily dropped his head into his hands.

"Tea, dear?" Emily asked calmly, waving the pot in Clarence's direction. "There's some nice sugar cookies if you'd like one. Just baked them myself. You look like you could use some refreshments." She turned to Molly. "How about you, dear? Would you like something?" She smiled and Molly's temper snapped. She reached out and took the pot from her aunt's hand, setting it down on the table with a bang.

"What I want," Molly said through clenched teeth, "is an explanation. *Right now.*" She dropped an arm around her aunt's shoulders. "Would you all excuse us, please?" Molly guided her aunt through the dining room and into the next room, which turned out to be a kitchen. A warm, cheerful kitchen. Shutting the swinging door behind her, Molly turned to her aunt.

"Now, would you mind telling me what the devil you're doing?" she cried. Whatever was going on was not funny. She had been genuinely frightened to discover her aunt gone. And now Aunt Emily was acting as if her disappearing was a perfectly natural occurrence.

"I already told you what I was doing," Emily said primly, as she sat down. "I was pouring tea."

Molly's eyes narrowed, and she glared at her aunt. "That's not what I mean, and you know it." Her voice rose, and she struggled to control herself. After mentally counting to ten, she continued. "What are you doing here? And why are all your clothes gone? You certainly don't need your entire wardrobe to play your weekly game of bridge."

Emily patted the seat next to her. "Maybe you'd better sit down, dear."

Yanking the chair out, Molly reluctantly sat down. She'd stand on her head if it meant getting a straight answer from her aunt. "All right, I'm sitting. Now let's have it. And from the beginning," she warned, narrowing her gaze.

"What would you like to know, dear?" Emily smiled.

Molly rolled her eyes heavenward and shook her head in despair. "Aunt Emily," she began slowly, with infinitely more patience than she felt. "You scared ten years off my life, and I want to know why! And don't tell me it was so you could pour tea for Ralph Pritchard. Certainly the man can handle that little chore by himself."

Emily's face fell. "Oh dear, I didn't mean to frighten you." She reached out and patted Molly's arm in a soothing gesture, but Molly wasn't soothed. "I was going to tell you—I tried to explain this morning, but, well, you were so upset, so I thought it could wait."

"What could wait?" Molly cried in exasperation. "What were you going to tell me?" She was going to scream if she didn't get some answers soon.

Emily smiled. "I've left you, dear."

"What!" Molly cried, lunging from the chair to stare at her aunt incredulously. "What do you mean, you've left me?" This was going a bit too far, even for her aunt.

Emily folded her hands primly on the table and coolly met Molly's startled gaze. "I've flown the coop! I've left you, dear!" Emily announced, obviously quite delighted with the idea.

Molly numbly shook her head and slumped back in her chair. None of this was making any sense. Struggling to control her temper, which was rising by the

moment, Molly took a deep breath, determined to try
again. "Aunt Emily," she said slowly, drawing her
words out carefully. "Would you mind telling me exactly what you're talking about?"

"Dear—" Emily frowned "—I thought I just did!
I've left you. I'm not going to live with you anymore."
She smiled. "Now, don't worry, I had the title to the
house changed to your name, so it's all legal." Emily
looked quite pleased with herself, and Molly wondered
if this little bit of information was supposed to make her
feel better.

"Aunt Emily," Molly cried. "I don't want the house.
I don't want anything except for you to come home and
stop talking nonsense."

"Molly, I am home." She reached out and covered
Molly's hand with hers. "This is my home now."

Molly closed her eyes and rubbed her aching temples. "Aunt Emily, this is Alma's home."

"And mine. And Ralph's."

Lord give me strength, Molly thought, closing her
eyes for a moment. She had the distinct feeling she was
not communicating with her aunt. At least they didn't
seem to be talking about the same subject.

"What do you mean this is your home, and Ralph
and Alma's?"

"Dear, I do wish you'd pay attention. If you calm
down, you might be able to understand what I'm saying so I wouldn't have to repeat myself."

Calm down? Molly glared at her aunt. Pigs would fly
before she calmed down unless she got some answers.
Some sensible answers. And soon.

"I'll calm down, Aunt Emily, if you promise to start
at the beginning and tell me why I came home to find

Clarence hysterical on my doorstep and you gone, along with all of your belongings."

Emily heaved an exasperated sigh. "I already told you. I've moved out."

Molly threw up her hands. "Aunt Emily!"

"Now don't get riled up, dear. Let me finish. The past few years I've been worried about you. You've been so alone, with no one but me and that silly cat for company. I know how hurt you were when Paul broke up with you," she added softly, patting Molly's hand.

"He didn't break up with me," Molly interjected, wanting once and for all to clear the air. If Aunt Emily was doing this based on some idea that she was still pining away for Paul, it was time to set the record straight.

Emily shook her head. "It doesn't matter who broke up with who. I know why." She stared pointedly at Molly, and in that instant Molly realized that perhaps her aunt did know the real reason. Emily cocked her head and smiled wisely. "Not much goes on that I don't know about, dear. Friend of mine owns Sunnydale Acres. I knew what that Paul Host was up to probably before you did." Emily gave an unladylike snort. "Do you really think I'd go live in some home just because that nervous little creep wanted me to?"

"You knew?" Molly was dumbfounded. All this time, Aunt Emily had known!

"'Course, I knew. Soon as Paul started making inquiries, my friend let me know." Emily chuckled softly. "We had some conversation, we did."

"Why didn't you ever say anything?"

"For what? You forget, child, I raised you. I knew exactly how you'd react," she added confidently. "If I had told you what that man was really like, you'd never have believed me. Some things you have to experience for yourself, dear." Emily's eyes darkened. "Never did like that boy. 'Miss Emily this, Miss Emily that.'" She mimicked Paul quite effectively, and Molly burst out laughing.

"Oh, Aunt Emily, I love you." Molly's voice was choked with emotion.

"I love you, too, dear," she said sweetly, "but it's about time for you to start living your own life, and for me to start living mine. That's why I've moved out." Her voice dropped to a whisper. "Alma's not as young as she used to be. Jonathan's been a mite worried about her living all alone in that house with the steps and all. Ralph and I and Alma are all going to live in this place together. Plenty of room. We can keep each other company, and maybe I'll finally be able to teach that man how to play a decent game of bridge."

Molly's head snapped up at the mention of Jonathan. "You mean Jonathan—" She stopped as a few of the puzzle pieces fell into place. "Is that what Jonathan's been working on for his grandmother?" Her eyes widened in surprise.

Emily nodded. "Of course, dear. That's why he came home. He handled the sale of Alma's old house and the purchase of this one. Even took care of deeding over my house to you."

Molly's throat constricted with regret. So this was what Jonathan had been working on! His words came back to haunt her. "I want only the best for my grandmother. My intentions are honorable. I came home to lend a hand and assist her." The words echoed through her mind, bringing a flush of shame.

"Oh, Aunt Emily," she moaned, dropping her face into her hands, "why didn't you just tell me you wanted to move out?'' Molly lifted her head and stared blankly at her aunt. Why hadn't Jonathan told her?

"Wasn't going to at first. I didn't want to leave you all alone. What else did you have in this world but me and that cat?'' Emily wrinkled her nose.

"What changed your mind?'' Molly asked softly.

"Your pigheadedness!'' Emily declared firmly. "You're a beautiful, wonderful woman, but you're as stubborn as the day is long. Why do you think I kept trying to fix you up with dates? I wanted you to find a man, someone to spend your life with. Wanted you to have someone to love, so I could get on with my life. You know, dear, I'm not getting any younger, and I would like to spend the few years I have left doing what I want to do.''

"Oh, Aunt Emily—'' Molly wiped a tear from her cheek and leaned over to hug her aunt ''—I love you. You don't have to worry about me. I'll be fine.''

"I don't want you to be fine, dear. I want you to be happy. Jonathan loves you and you love him. You're determined to believe that Jonathan betrayed you.'' Emily looked at her tenderly. "If you'd give that poor boy a chance to explain, you'd realize he didn't.''

For the first time, Molly began to realize she might have been wrong about Jonathan. Was there a valid reason for what had happened at the village hall meeting? A shadow of doubt weaved a path through her tormented thoughts.

"What about the senior center?'' Had her aunt forgotten about that?

"I already told you, Molly, you've got to give that boy a chance to explain.'' Emily smiled tenderly. "He loves you, dear. He's a good boy.''

Molly thought about her aunt's words. She had been wrong. So wrong about Jonathan. Was it possible there was an explanation for what had happened last night? There was only one way to find out.

"I know what I'm going to do with the rest of my life, Molly. What are you going to do with yours?"

Molly looked at her aunt in silence for a moment, her heart and mind fighting an age-old battle. Her heart won out. She had to give Jonathan a chance to explain. Her aunt had been right this morning; she did owe Jonathan that much.

Emily's eyes danced merrily. "If you hurry, you may be able to catch him."

Molly jumped from the chair. "Aunt Emily, I love you. I'm sure you'll be very happy here." She threw her arms around her aunt and hugged her tight. Aunt Emily was right. It was time to go on, for both of them. Time to go forward and build a future. A future Molly wanted to share with a laughing redheaded giant.

Emily followed Molly back into the dining room, where Ralph and Clarence were still engaged in a heated discussion.

"Where's Jonathan?" Molly asked.

"But Daddy, what will people think? You living in sin with two women you're not married to?" Clarence's voice was hushed, and he was staring at his father, wide-eyed. "What will people say?"

"Plenty," Ralph returned with a chuckle. "It'll give 'em something to talk about."

"Where's Jonathan?" she repeated, but they paid no attention to her. Finally her eyes found Alma. "Alma, where is he?" she cried in exasperation.

Alma smiled. "Probably at my old house. Had a few last minute things to do. If you hurry, you might be able to catch him."

"Clarence, can I use the squad car?"

Clarence abruptly stopped talking and stared at her as if she had asked him for his last breath. "Now, Miss Molly, you know that's an official law-enforcement vehicle. Only authorized personnel are allowed to use that car."

Molly took a threatening step toward him. Authorized personnel, indeed! Ralph picked up the keys from the table and tossed them to Molly. "Here you go, missy. Help yourself."

She flashed him a grateful smile. "Thanks, Ralph." Impulsively she bent and brushed his cheek with her lips. "You're terrific." She whirled and yanked open the door. Time was wasting. She had to find Jonathan.

"Daddy, you shouldn't have done that. No one but me and Junior are supposed to drive the squad car."

"Hush up, boy." Emily pushed him back down in the chair. "Have a cookie."

Sliding into the driver's seat, Molly flipped on the siren and stepped on the gas. She wheeled the squad car up and down the familiar streets, keeping an eye open for Jonathan. She had to find him, had to give him a chance to explain.

She had been so wrong. She had doubted him and condemned him. A heavy sigh lifted her shoulders. Would he be able to forgive her? she wondered as she turned a corner. He had to; she loved him. And, she thought with a wicked smile, if he gave her half a chance, she'd show him just how much.

With a screech, she slammed on the brakes in front of his grandmother's old house and flipped off the si-

ren. He had to have heard her coming. The whole town
had probably heard her.

She jumped from the car and raced up the walk. A
sudden thought jarred her, and a smile lit her face.
Tipping her head back, she cupped her hands over her
mouth. "Yo, Jon-a-than!"

It wasn't necessary to repeat the call. The front door
opened, and Jonathan leaned indolently against the
doorframe. His eyes met hers and she grinned broadly.
He stared at her for a moment, and then, finally, his lips
curved in a boyish smile.

"The whole town will be talking," he scolded good-
naturedly, crossing his arms across his chest.

"I know." She smiled back, basking in the warmth
of him.

"Think of your reputation," he teased.

"I don't have to. Everyone else in town thinks about
it for me."

He cocked his head and looked at her skeptically.
"Does Clarence know you've got his car?"

"Well, yes and no." She grinned. "Clarence knows,
but he didn't exactly give me permission."

"Molly Margaret Maguire, do you mean to tell me
that 'Miss Emily's poor spinster niece' has resorted to
stealing cars?" Jonathan's brows rose and his eyes
twinkled.

"It's all right." Her grin widened, and she took another step closer. "I know a good lawyer."

"I love you, Molly." He stepped out of the doorway
and walked slowly toward her.

"I love you, too." She took a step forward, her heart
soaring. "Last night I—"

"Last night, you didn't let me finish," he scolded
gently. "I think the center *should* be torn down. It's

unsafe. But I managed to convince the owners of the new shopping mall to allocate two thousand square feet of office space, rent free, for a new senior center.''

Tears filled her eyes as she flew into his arms. "Oh, Jonathan, I'm sorry. I'm so sorry. Can you forgive me for not trusting you?" She lifted her head and met his gaze. She drank in the sight of him, afraid he might disappear.

"That depends," he said, holding her at arm's length. "You once told me you were your own woman. Still feel the same way?"

She gazed up at him. He was doing it again. Overwhelming her. But she loved it. "Yes," she murmured, snuggling closer to him. "Why?"

"How would you feel about marrying a temporarily unemployed attorney?"

Molly's eyes widened. "You lost your job?"

He shook his head and laughed softly. "I didn't lose it, honey. I know exactly where it's at." He waited for her frown before he continued. "I quit."

"You quit your job? Why?"

Jonathan slid his arms around her waist and pulled her close to him, groaning softly with desire as her slim frame molded against him. "Portland is too far away from the three most important ladies in my life. Besides, I've always wanted to go into private practice in a small town." He bent his head and let his lips trail slowly across her upturned face.

Molly blinked and looked up at him. "Three women?" she echoed weakly.

"Yes, three," he murmured huskily, dipping his mouth to kiss her. "Grandmother, Aunt Emily and you."

"Oh, Jonathan, that's wonderful." She hugged him tightly, not caring that they were standing in the middle of town in broad daylight. She laid her head on his shoulder, suddenly filled with a wonderful peace.

"Molly—" he tipped her chin to look at her "—you know, you never did answer my question." He dropped his mouth over hers and drank of her sweetness.

"Question?" she murmured, pulling her mouth from his. She was going to have to get used to Jonathan's abrupt changes of subject. But that wouldn't be too difficult; she'd had lots of practice with her aunt. Dear, beloved Aunt Emily. Molly smiled; her aunt had finally found her "a good one."

"What question?" she asked, snuggling closer.

"Do you need a man in your life?" Jonathan asked softly, his eyes filled with love.

"You're the only man I'll ever need," she said huskily, burying her face in the warmth of his neck.

"Molly," he croaked, holding her away from him, "then would you please put me out of my misery and say you'll marry me?"

Giving him a wicked smile, Molly stepped out of his arms and raised her head to the early afternoon sun. She opened her mouth and shouted for all she was worth, hoping the whole town could hear.

"Now hear this! Miss Emily's poor spinster niece is not going to be a poor spinster anymore." Her heart sang and her toes curled as she walked back into Jonathan's waiting arms.

Epilogue

Miss Molly Margaret Maguire and Mr. Jonathan Kent were married this morning in Hillchester Chapel. The bride was attended by her aunt, Miss Emily Maguire, and by the groom's grandmother, Mrs. Alma Kent. Both ladies were resplendent in their identical lavender floor-length gowns with matching straw hats. Ralph Pritchard, father of Sheriff Pritchard, gave the beaming bride away. Twins, Mark and Martha Simpson, served as ring bearer and flower girl, while their mother, Mrs. Shirley Simpson, took the wedding pictures.

After a honeymoon at an undisclosed location, the newlyweds plan to reside in Hillchester, where Mr. Kent will be opening a private law practice.

(This reporter learned from an exclusive source that Mr. Kent's first client was to be his new wife, Molly, who had been charged with unlawful use of a municipal vehicle. Rumor has it that a deal was made, and the charges against Molly Maguire Kent have been dropped.)

"Molly? Are you still awake?"

"Hmm?" Nuzzling closer to her new husband, Molly slid her bare leg over his.

"Molly?" Jonathan sat up and leaned back against the headboard, carefully keeping an arm around her. "We made the front page of the paper. Listen." He slowly read the piece to her.

Molly lazily opened one eye and looked at him quizzically. "*Did* you get Clarence to drop the charges?"

Jonathan chuckled softly. "Sure did."

Molly snuggled closer to him. "How on earth did you manage that?"

Jonathan chuckled again. "We traded. I gave Clarence something he wanted. And he gave me something I wanted."

A suspicious smile curved her mouth. "What on earth did you have that Clarence wanted?"

Jonathan's grin widened. "Nickodemus."

Molly bolted upright. "You gave Clarence my cat!"

Jonathan pulled her back down into the circle of his arms. "Honey," he said softly, bending his his head to nuzzle her neck. "Clarence was lonely without his father."

Molly sighed with pleasure as Jonathan's mouth captured hers, sending her heart into spasms of joy. She slid her arms around his neck just as he pulled his lips from hers.

Molly frowned in the darkness. "Jonathan Kent! Is that it?"

Jonathan groaned softly. "No, Molly girl," he whispered. "That's just the beginning."

COMING NEXT MONTH

FAMILY AFFAIR—Rita Rainville
Brady wanted to marry the right woman—Sara Clayton. And
with the help of five elderly friends and one orangutan, he set out
to win her love.

GIFT OF THE GODS—Judith McWilliams
Rescuing her teenage "charge" from the hands of wealthy Greek
Philip Stephanos turned out to be easier than rescuing herself—
especially when Sophie discovered she didn't want to be rescued!

A MAN FOR SYLVIA—Sue Santore
What was the mystery of the velvet painting? Could it be behind
the accidents befalling Sylvia? With Craig's help, Sylvia probed
the puzzling secrets of the picture—and her heart.

THE FOREVER KIND—Karen Young
When Jill's little boy disappeared, it was old friend
Sam Halloran to the rescue. But finding Josh was easier than
convincing Jill to take another chance on love—and Sam.

FOR EACH TOMORROW—Curtiss Ann Matlock
It had been years since Quent left town. Now he was back—a
dashing Oklahoma Ranger—and after Cassie's heart. Cassie
didn't want to give it to him. But she soon learned that in order to
gain, you had to risk—and that the reward was worth the price.

NO QUESTIONS ASKED—Lynnette Morland
Conn Tomelty, celebrated journalist, was doing a story on
Lifeline, a disaster relief organization. But what he really wanted
to research was its newly appointed director, Rosalie Madden.

AVAILABLE THIS MONTH

UNLIKELY LOVER
Diana Palmer

THE CASTAWAYS
Frances Lloyd

FRIENDS—AND THEN SOME
Debbie Macomber

HEAVENLY MATCH
Sharon De Vita

THE EYES OF A STRANGER
Terri McGraw

HERO ON HOLD
Glenda Sands

Silhouette Desire

**Available
January 1987**

NEVADA
SILVER

The third book in the exciting
Desire Trilogy by Joan Hohl.

The Sharp brothers are back, along with
sister Kit . . . and Logan McKittrick.

Kit's loved Logan all her life and, with a little
help from the silver glow of a Nevada night,
she must convince the stubborn rancher that
she's a woman who needs a man's love—not
the protection of another brother.

Don't miss *Nevada Silver*—Kit and
Logan's story and the conclusion
of Joan Hohl's acclaimed
Desire Trilogy.

Silhouette Special Edition

Sophisticated and moving,
these expanded romances delight
and capture your imagination
book after book.
A rich mix of complex plots,
realism and adventure.

SIL-SE-1RR